Also by Alex Morgan

ALEX MORGAN

Simon & Schuster Books for Young Readers
New York   London   Toronto   Sydney   New Delhi

SIMON & SCHUSTER BOOKS FOR YOUNG READERS

An imprint of Simon & Schuster Children's Publishing Division

1230 Avenue of the Americas, New York, New York 10020

This book is a work of fiction. Any references to historical events, real people, or real places are used fictitiously. Other names, characters, places, and events are products of the author's imagination, and any resemblance to actual events or places or persons, living or dead, is entirely coincidental.

Text © 2020 by Full Fathom Five

Cover illustration © 2020 by Paula Franco

All rights reserved, including the right of reproduction in whole or in part in any form.

SIMON & SCHUSTER BOOKS FOR YOUNG READERS

and related marks are trademarks of Simon & Schuster, Inc.

For information about special discounts for bulk purchases, please contact Simon & Schuster Special Sales at 1-866-506-1949 or business@simonandschuster.com.

The Simon & Schuster Speakers Bureau can bring authors to your live event. For more information or to book an event, contact the Simon & Schuster Speakers Bureau at 1-866-248-3049 or visit our website at www.simonspeakers.com.

Also available in a Simon & Schuster Books for Young Readers hardcover edition

Interior design by Tom Daly

The text for this book was set in Berling.

Manufactured in the United States of America

0221 OFF

First Simon & Schuster Books for Young Readers paperback edition March 2021

2 4 6 8 10 9 7 5 3 1

The Library of Congress has cataloged the hardcover edition as follows:

Names: Morgan, Alex (Alexandra Patricia), 1989– author.

Title: Homecoming / Alex Morgan.

Description: First edition. | New York : Simon & Schuster Books for Young Readers, [2020] | Series: The Kicks | Audience: Ages 8–12. | Audience: Grades 4–6. | Summary: Devin visits her best friend, Kara, in Connecticut but the visit goes very badly, distracting Devin just before the Kicks' first playoff match.

Identifiers: LCCN 2019035942 | ISBN 9781534428065 (hardcover) | ISBN 9781534428072 (paperback) | ISBN 9781534428089 (ebook)

Subjects: CYAC: Friendship—Fiction. | Soccer—Fiction.

Classification: LCC PZ7.M818 Hom 2020 | DDC [Fic]—dc23

LC record available at https://lccn.loc.gov/2019035942

CHAPTER ONE

Adrenaline pumped through my body as I raced down the field. One of the Marlins was dribbling at rocket speed toward the Kicks goal, and none of our defending midfielders could catch up to her. With her hands on her knees in front of the goal, Emma waited for the ball, eyes alert. The score was tied, 17–17, and the clock was running down.

Wham! The Marlin kicked the ball hard. Emma lunged for it, and it bounced off her gloved hands, careening back onto the field. The same player got control of it again.

My friend Frida, a Kicks defender, charged up to her. Frida was an actor who pretended to be different characters to gain courage on the soccer field. Today she was a pirate.

"Aaargh. We shall give no quarter to thieves who try to steal our pirate gold!" she yelled.

Frida's strange cry startled the Marlin, who stumbled just enough for Frida to kick the ball away from her. It went flying and landed between another Marlin and Zoe, who got to it first, which was not a surprise because she had some of the fastest moves I've ever seen. She dribbled toward the Marlins' goal, with the player who missed out on the ball at her heels.

I changed direction to get clear in case Zoe wanted to pass. She kicked it right to me just as the player behind her caught up to her.

I got control of the ball and dribbled into Marlin territory. In twenty feet I'd be close enough to shoot . . .

I saw a turquoise-and-white blur out of the corner of my left eye. One of the Marlins was coming at me fast. I turned and saw another defender charging toward me from the front.

"Devin! Over here!"

Jessi called to me from my right. I turned to face her and saw that she was clear.

Wham! I sent the ball skidding across the grass. Jessi stopped it and zoomed toward the goal. I could hear our fans screaming in the stands.

"Go, Jessi!"

"Go, Kicks!"

Jessi got within range and sent the ball soaring. I stopped, watching it fly through the air. The Marlins goalie jumped up to block it, but she fell short. It grazed the top of her fingers and slammed into the net.

The ref blew her whistle. *Game over!*

"The Kicks win!" somebody shouted.

I ran to Jessi and slapped her on the back. "You were awesome!"

She grinned at me. "*We* were awesome, you mean," she said. "Thanks for setting me up."

"No problem," I said.

We ran to line up with the rest of our teammates, to slap hands with the Marlins. I knew how much it hurt to lose— especially when a game was that close—and I could see the disappointment on their faces.

After I slapped the last palm, I jogged back to the sideline where the Kicks were gathering. When everyone arrived, we huddled in a circle, jumping up and down with excitement.

"Great game, everybody!" congratulated Grace, an eighth grader and my co-captain.

Coach Flores approached us, and we broke up the circle.

"Good work, girls!" she said. "This means we've made the playoffs!"

We began yelling and cheering.

"You all certainly earned it," Coach continued as we quieted down. "The first playoff game is in two weeks, so our practice schedule is going to change a bit. Our weekday practices will continue. But there's a break next weekend, with no regular games, so we'll practice at ten a.m. that Saturday."

Megan, another eighth grader, raised her hand. "Do we know who we're playing in the first game?"

Coach shook her head. "No, but we'll know when all of

today's games are finished. I'll send out a group text when I get the word."

"This is great news," said Grace. "Let's go to Pizza Kitchen to celebrate!"

Everybody started packing up their water bottles and duffel bags. Jessi, Emma, Zoe, Frida, and I gravitated toward one another as we got ready to go. We all looked like kind of a mess, except for Zoe, who always managed to look neat and whose short, blond hair kept her head cool when she played. Jessi's long braids helped with the heat, too, but like me, her jersey was soaked with sweat. Frida's curly auburn hair was falling out of the high bun she'd had it in, and Emma's arms and legs were streaked with dirt from her diving after the ball.

"That game was intense, and I'm starving!" Jessi said. "I'm going to eat a whole pizza by myself."

"I'm pretty hungry too," Zoe said. "Want to split a veggie pizza with me when we get there, Devin?"

"I can't go, remember?" I said. "I've got to go get my dress for Charlotte's party."

"Aw, come on. That's, like, a week away," Jessi said. "We made the playoffs! You have to celebrate with us!"

"I know, but Sabine is helping me pick it out, and this is the only time she's free," I explained.

"You know, I should be insulted that you didn't ask *me*," Zoe said. "But Sabine is flawless, so I understand."

"Oh, no!" I said. "I told Sabine I was going to a sweet sixteen party, so she offered to take me shopping, but I should've totally thought to ask you. I'm sorry."

"Don't worry about it," Zoe replied. "Just send us a picture so we can see how gorgeous you look, okay?"

"I promise," I said, and I glanced at Jessi. By her frowny face I knew she was upset that I wasn't going to celebrate our big win.

I hugged her.

"Go get your pizza. I'll be there in spirit," I told her.

"I'll make sure to eat an extra slice for you," Jessi promised, and I knew that everything was good between us.

I headed back home with Mom, Dad, and Maisie, who had come to cheer me on at the game because they're awesome. I showered and changed into shorts and a T-shirt when I got home, a fitting outfit for an 80-degree day. It was that warm even though it was still spring. That wasn't unusual for Southern California, but it was my first spring living here. Almost a year before, my family had moved here from Connecticut, and less than a week from now I was heading back for a few days.

My best friend in Connecticut was Kara. She and I talked almost every day, and I still missed her. I missed seeing her at school and playing on the same soccer team. It helped that I'd made some new best friends here in California, but I wished Kara could be part of my life here too.

When Kara and I were in third grade, an older girl named Charlotte was our soccer mentor. Now Charlotte was turning sixteen and she had invited both me and Kara to come to her sweet sixteen party. I had thought that I wouldn't be able to go, but then Dad had found out he had to go back to Connecticut for a meeting, and he'd said he'd bring me with him.

I was kind of excited to be going back to Connecticut, and totally psyched for Charlotte's party. I was less excited when Kara told me I needed to find a semiformal dress for it, though, because fashion was not my thing. That was when Sabine had offered to help.

Sabine and I had met on a modeling job. For a hot second I'd done some photo shoots for sports fashions, until I'd decided that modeling wasn't for me.

The best thing about it was meeting Sabine. She modeled too, but she went to another school, so I never would have met her if I hadn't done those gigs.

When I was ready, Mom drove me to the mall to meet Sabine.

"Text me when you find a dress you like, and I'll come check it out," Mom told me as we walked to the fountain in the center of the mall. "I need to find a new yoga mat."

Sabine was waiting for us by the fountain.

"Devin!" she called out, and I swear her perfect white teeth gleamed when she smiled at me. Zoe was right—Sabine was flawless, without a hair out of place or a pimple on her smooth, brown skin. Thanks to a daily combination of sweat and sunscreen, three bright red pimples had popped up on my pale white chin just that morning.

"Hey, Sabine," I said. "Thanks for helping me find a dress!"

"Yes, thanks," my mom said. "Please guide Devin toward

something youthful and tasteful? And not too short?"

"Mom!" I said.

"Don't worry, Mrs. Burke," Sabine said. "I actually have the perfect dress picked out already. I think you'll like it."

"Terrific! Devin will text me once you've figured it out," Mom said, and then she waved and took off.

"Congrats on winning your game today," Sabine said.

"Thanks—wait. How did you know?" I asked.

"Zoe texted me," she replied.

"Oh, right," I said. After I'd told Zoe about Sabine, they'd connected on social media. I knew they had a lot in common, and I'd had a hunch that they could be friends. It sounded like they'd clicked pretty fast—so I'd been right!

"How was your photo shoot yesterday?" I asked.

Sabine rolled her eyes. "It went on for *hours*," she said. "The client was there, and she kept telling the photographer what I should do, and she kept changing her mind. 'Smile. Don't smile! Smile. Don't smile!'" Sabine shook her head. "I think I pulled a mouth muscle."

I laughed. "I'm glad I decided to stick to soccer," I told her.

"I get it. But, Devin, you were *good*," she said. "Anyway, you need to model one more time, in this dress I picked out. Come on."

She took my hand, and I followed her through the packed mall. We ended up at a big shop called Belle of the Ball, with lots of fancy dresses in the window. My eyes widened.

"These look like runway gowns," I said. "Are you sure I'm supposed to wear something like this?"

"This shop has semiformal dresses too, and I found one that will work perfectly. Trust me," Sabine said.

She led me through the shop to a rack of dresses and pulled out a light blue one with little sparkly stones scattered across it that reminded me of stars.

"The blue goes with your eyes," she said. "Try it on!"

I obeyed and tried on the dress in the changing room. It was sleeveless, with a straight neckline and a skirt that went out at the waist. I looked at myself in the mirror. The skirt hit right at my knee—not too short, just like Mom had asked for. Even with my pimples, and my skinned knee from practice, I thought I looked beautiful.

I swung my arms, and then I did a twirl. The dress was comfortable, too! It was amazing!

"Come on, Devin!" Sabine urged from outside the curtain.

I stepped out of the changing booth, and Sabine smiled widely. "It's spectacular! You look gorgeous!"

"I love it," I admitted. "In fact, I don't think I've ever looked this good in anything. You are a genius!"

"When I was scoping out the dresses, I just knew this was the one," she said.

I went back into the booth, took out my phone, and gave it to her. "Can you take my picture, please?"

"Sure," she said. She held up the phone. "Let's see some model poses, Devin. Smile! Don't smile! Now smile!"

I stuck my tongue out at her. "Very funny," I said. I took the phone from her. "But thank you."

I texted Mom the picture and the name of the store, and by the time I had changed back into my shorts and shirt, she was at the register, waiting for us.

"I love it!" she said. "Thank you so much, Sabine."

"You're welcome," Sabine replied. "I had a good time."

Mom paid for the dress and then took me and Sabine to the salad place for a late lunch. Then we dropped Sabine off at her house on our way home.

I walked into our house, clutching the bag with my dress in it. Weird, I know, but it was the first time I'd ever been in love with an item of clothing.

Maisie ran up to me. "Let me see it! Let me see it!"

I set the bag down on the coffee table and carefully pulled out the dress. Maisie's eyes went wide.

"It's a fairy princess dress!" she exclaimed. She turned to Mom. "How come Devin gets a fairy princess dress and I don't?"

"When you have a special event to go to, I will get you a fairy princess dress," Mom promised.

Maisie frowned. "How come Devin gets to go to a special event and I don't?"

Mom sighed. "Maisie, we've been over this."

I put the dress back into the bag and ran up the stairs, two at a time.

"Thanks, Mom! I'm going to show Kara!" I called behind me.

I ran into my room and closed the door. First I texted Kara the picture of me in the dress. Then I turned on my laptop and called her on video chat.

After a few beeps her face appeared on the screen.

"That dress is amazing!" she said. "Devin, I'm so excited!"

I held up the dress so she could see it again. "I know!" I said. "I'm excited too."

"My parents are getting me out of school early on Thursday so we can pick you and your dad up from the airport," Kara said, talking quickly. "And Friday I'm taking off from school and we're going to do something special, but it's a surprise. And we have practice before the party on Saturday night and you can come and watch. And—"

"Okay. Slow down. You're going to make my head explode!" I teased. "Trust me, I'm really excited to be going back ho—"

I stopped myself from saying "home." Connecticut used to be my home, but it wasn't anymore.

"We're going to have an awesome time," Kara promised. "Hey, I have to help make dinner. I'll see you in five days."

"Five days!" I replied, and then we ended the call. I was all happy and floaty.

The Kicks were going to the playoffs. I was going back to Connecticut to see Kara. And I was going to wear a beautiful dress and go to an awesome party.

I do feel like a fairy princess, I thought, and then I heard Jessi's voice in my head.

Really, Devin? What's next, are you going to grow wings?

I laughed, but then I got a little bit sad, thinking about how I would miss Jessi while I was visiting Kara.

But it was only for a few days.

CHAPTER TWO

"Only three more days of Devin," Emma said with a sigh. Then she popped a piece of cucumber sushi roll into her mouth. (Emma's mom packed her the most amazing lunches every day.)

My friends and I were eating in the cafeteria of Kentville Middle School. Today we'd scored a table outside in the beautiful Southern California sunshine.

"I'm not going away forever," I told her. "It's only for a few days. You won't even miss me."

"Of course we will!" Zoe said.

"We'll miss you at practice," Jessi added. "Especially since I found out that we're playing the Eagles in our first game. They're a strong team."

"Didn't we beat them?" I asked.

Jessi shook her head. "Nope. That was the day the eighth graders pretended to be sick and stayed home. Remember?"

The details of the game came flooding back to me. It

had been a hot day down at the Victorton field, and we'd had a hard time getting through the Eagles' defense. I started to sweat now, just thinking about it, but the heat wasn't why we had lost. We couldn't beat them because some of our strongest players had been missing.

"Well, that's not going to happen again," Emma pointed out. "The eighth graders only did that because they were mad at us. But everything's good now. We're all getting along."

"Still, we don't really know if we can beat them," Jessi said. "That's why we need to practice harder than ever. *All* of us." She looked at me.

"I'm only missing two practices," I said. "I'll be back in time for practice on Monday. That's plenty of time to get ready for the playoffs."

"Good," Jessi said. "Because I want to go all the way this time."

Everyone got quiet, remembering the playoffs at the end of the fall season. We had won the first two games, getting the league championship. But our bid for state had ended with a painful loss to the Brightville Bolts.

"This is way different from the fall season," I pointed out. "Going into the playoffs, we weren't playing as a team. Then Coach Flores's dad got sick, and Coach Valentine replaced her."

Frida shuddered. "I still have nightmares. He was so strict!"

"I think he was a good coach, but it threw us off our game," I said.

"Don't forget that the Kicks couldn't even win until you came along, Devin," Emma added.

I blushed. "You were always a good team. You just . . ."

"We needed a push in the right direction, and you gave it to us," Zoe finished for me. "Honestly, Devin, I don't know where we'd be if you hadn't moved here."

"Yeah. Sorry, Connecticut—we need Devin here!" Emma said.

"Well, we're a strong team now," I said. "We're in a groove. We're playing really well together. I have a good feeling about the playoffs."

Emma turned to Frida. "Ooh, check that fortune-telling app! Ask it if the Kicks will become state champs!"

Frida frowned. "Oh, I took that app off my phone," she said. "My agent told me they're cutting me out of the commercial. So Flash Fortune is dead to me!"

I felt bad for Frida. She had been so excited to book that acting gig.

"It's their loss," I said. "Sorry."

Frida shrugged. "That's show business," she replied. "As Miriam says, when one door closes, another opens."

Miriam used to be a movie star a long time ago, and she and Frida were friends. I was pretty sure that Frida was going to be a movie star one day, just like Miriam had been.

"Well, I don't want some app to tell me what's going to happen in the playoffs, anyway," Jessi said. "I want to work hard, and win."

"I'll be at practice tonight and Wednesday," I told her. "Then we're flying out Thursday morning."

"When's the party? Saturday?" Emma asked.

I nodded.

"A sweet sixteen party sounds like fun," Emma added.

"I'm so glad I get to go," I said. "And I get to see some of my old friends too."

Zoe grinned. "They're not going to recognize you in that gorgeous dress, Devin."

I had texted a picture of the dress to everyone—which was *so* not like me at all. But I was really in love with it!

I laughed. "It hasn't even been a year. I'm sure they'll recognize me."

"I don't know," Emma said. "You're, like, a lot taller than when you moved here. And your hair used to be just brown, but now you've got blond streaks in it from the sun."

"Yup," Jessi agreed. "You totally look like a California girl, not a Connecticut girl."

"Connecticut girls and California girls don't look much different," I said.

Frida stood up, pulling a banana from her lunch bag. She leaned across the table and tapped me on the left shoulder, then the right, and finally on the top of my head.

"We claim thee as a citizen of California!" she announced. "You are hereby given permission to travel to Connecticut for four days. But then you must return."

I laughed. "I have to. I've already got my plane ticket back."

"Promise you'll text us pictures of the party?" Zoe asked.

"And Connecticut's near Manhattan, isn't it?" Frida

asked. "Take pictures if you go there. I'm dying to visit Broadway one day."

"Devin's still got two more practices," Jessi reminded everyone. "She's not leaving yet."

"That's right!" I said.

For the next three days it was hard to focus on anything except my upcoming trip. Soccer took my mind off it, but after Wednesday's practice I launched into full trip-prep mode with Mom. Wednesday night she rummaged through my open suitcase.

"Do you have your pajamas? Another pair of sweatpants for the plane ride back? Extra underwear?"

"It's all there, Mom," I promised her. "I followed your list."

I held up the list she had printed out for me.

Mom took the paper and examined it, frowning. "Deodorant . . . sunscreen . . . toothpaste," she muttered. "What are we forgetting? I feel like we're forgetting something."

"We're not forgetting anything," I assured her. I patted my dress, folded in half on top of the suitcase. "I've got the shoes for this, and the necklace you lent me is in the little pocket on the side."

"Mrs. O'Connell said she'll steam the dress for you before the party, in case it gets wrinkled," Mom said. "You're going to get ready for the party at Kara's house."

I hugged her. "Thanks, Mom. You think of everything."

Mom squeezed me tightly. "I'm going to miss you, Devin."

"You and all of my friends!" I said. "I'm only going for a few days. It's no big deal."

Maisie poked her head in the doorway. "Well, *I'm* not going to miss you."

"Nobody asked you," I shot back.

"Girls! Don't get into a fight before Devin leaves," Mom scolded.

"I'm just being honest. You don't want me to be a *liar*, do you?" Maisie asked. "I won't miss Devin because she hogs the bathroom in the morning and she has her own computer and I don't."

"I need my laptop for school," I pointed out. "And anyway, that's not a good reason not to miss me."

"You two hug it out right now," Mom ordered. "And, Maisie, I think you *will* miss Devin and you're trying not to show it. It's better to share your feelings than keep them buried inside."

"Okay. Then, I *feel* that I won't miss Devin hogging the bathroom every morning," Maisie said.

Mom gave her a look, so Maisie hugged me, and I hugged her back. I wanted to tell her I was going to miss her, because deep down I knew I would, but I didn't want to give her the satisfaction.

"Good," Mom said. "Now, right to bed, Devin. Your dad is going to wake you up at four a.m."

I nodded. I knew the plan. After Mom and Maisie left, I zipped up my suitcase, hauled it off my bed, and climbed under the covers.

It was only eight thirty, so of course I didn't sleep! I scrolled through my phone until I felt sort of sleepy at ten, but even then I couldn't fall asleep right away. I was too excited about the trip! I finally drifted off, and right after that (at least, that's what it felt like), Dad shook me awake.

I woke up with a low groan, but I didn't complain. I had begged and plotted and pleaded to go on this trip, and I didn't want to be ungrateful. Dad carried my suitcase downstairs, and I quickly got dressed in blue sweats, a Kicks T-shirt, and sneakers. When I got to the kitchen, Dad was gulping a cup of coffee.

"The car will be here any minute," he said.

I nodded. It was too early to speak!

Five minutes later we saw a black car pull up in front of the house, and soon we were on our way to the airport. The sky was still dark, with only a hint of pale light on the horizon. There were more cars on the road than I'd thought there would be this early in the morning, but I guess that was the way it was in Southern California. Everybody was always trying to get somewhere!

The airport was more crowded than I'd imagined too. We had to weave through a sea of people to get to the baggage check-in line. We waited on that line for almost an hour. I yawned the whole time, but I tried not to complain. I was on my way to see Kara!

After we checked our bags, we waited on another line to get through security. Then we walked down a long, long corridor to get to our terminal, grabbing some breakfast sandwiches at a little fast food place on the way. Finally, we found seats and waited to board the plane. I had packed headphones with me, and I plugged them into my phone and listened to music, which put me right to sleep!

Dad shook me awake.

"Devin, it's time to board," he said, and I nodded sleepily. When we got onto the plane, Dad let me have the window seat and he took the middle seat, which was really nice of him. I buckled my seat belt and watched the safety video on the monitor screen attached to the back of the seat in front of me.

Then I closed my eyes and waited for takeoff. Instead I heard the captain's voice over the speakers.

"Ladies and gentlemen, we're being delayed at the gate," he announced. "We should be taking off in about a half hour or so."

I heard some people groan. I just kept my eyes closed and tried to sleep, but I couldn't. After what seemed like forever, the plane finally started to roll down the runway.

I'd flown in a plane a few times before, and I liked to fly—especially when I could look out the window. As the engines roared, I gazed outside and watched the world get smaller and smaller below. Very quickly we soared up into the clouds and the morning sun. The glare was so bright that I had to close my window shade.

Taking off and landing were always the most exciting parts of any airplane flight. The rest of the six-hour trip was pretty boring. The view from the window for most of the trip was a bank of endless, boring clouds. I ate a boring chicken sandwich for lunch. After three hours I got bored of listening to music. I was so bored, I couldn't even sleep!

When we reached JFK airport in New York, it was three thirty in the afternoon there, because we had changed time zones. I was so happy when the plane landed! We weaved our way through more crowds to the baggage claim area.

"I'm texting Jack now," Dad said. Jack was Kara's dad. "They're going to pull up outside baggage claim after we get our luggage."

I stared at the conveyer belt that moved around and around in a circle. I anxiously tapped my right foot while I waited for our things to appear. I couldn't wait to see Kara!

A loud buzzer went off, and bags began to drop onto the carousel. Big bags. Small bags. Black bags. Brown bags.

But not mine. Not Dad's.

"Dad, what's happening?" I asked.

"There are still more coming," Dad said. "Don't worry." But his voice sounded stressed.

We watched as people grabbed their luggage and stepped out into the parking area. We watched until the last bag dropped—and then no more came.

Dad ran a hand through his hair. "Come on. Let's go ask at the booth," he said.

I followed him to a booth, where he explained our situation to a woman with a computer. Dad handed her our claim ticket, and she typed in the numbers.

"Okay. Well, it looks like your bags are in Albuquerque," she said.

"Albuquerque?" Dad repeated.

I started to panic. All of my stuff was in that bag! My pajamas and underwear and toothbrush! And . . . my dress! My beautiful dress! Tears started to well up in my eyes.

"I apologize for the inconvenience, but we can have them delivered to you when they arrive here," the woman said. "Where are you staying?"

I tuned out Dad while he gave her the information. All of a sudden I felt exhausted and my stomach hurt and I wanted to sob. My bag was in Albuquerque, and here I was, hundreds and hundreds of miles away from home.

Dad put his arm around me. "Sorry, kiddo. This stinks. But airlines are usually good about this kind of thing. I bet we'll get our bags tomorrow."

I nodded silently, and Dad led me out into the parking area. Taxis and cars whizzed by. The air felt cold and smelled like exhaust. In the distance I saw a cold, gray sky.

"DEVIN!"

I turned to see Kara running toward me. She crashed into me and hugged me and started jumping up and down.

"Devin! Devin! Devin!"

At point I did start to cry, a mix of sad, exhausted, and happy tears—mostly happy.

I was reunited with my best friend!

CHAPTER THREE

"OMG! You're, like, a foot taller than me!" Kara squealed as she wrapped me in a hug so tight that I felt like I couldn't breathe.

"Oof!" I gasped. "If I've gotten taller, you've gotten stronger!"

Kara pulled back, her hands clutching my arms tightly. She gave them a squeeze that made me squeak.

"Sienna and I have been doing CrossFit at the gym her dad owns," Kara said. "I'm totally buff now, Devin."

We both laughed as I looked into her big blue eyes, which, whether she was buff or not, still looked super-sweet and kind.

"Is Sienna the new girl, the one who joined the Cosmos?" I asked.

"Yes! I totally friend suggested the two of you on Snapface. You'd really like each other," Kara answered.

"I must have missed that," I told her. "I've been super obsessed with getting us into the playoffs. I haven't been on social stuff a lot."

"And you made it!" Kara gave me another hug. "Now I can hug you in person to congratulate you, and we can celebrate tonight!"

Kara and I had been so wrapped up in each other that I almost didn't notice Kara's parents, Mr. and Mrs. O'Connell, who were talking with my dad.

"Are you still waiting for your bags?" asked Kara's mom.

"They're in Albquerque," Dad replied with a frown.

"Oh, dear!" Mrs. O'Connell said. "Don't worry. We'll help you figure this out. But first, I need a hug from Devin!"

Mrs. O'Connell wrapped her arms around me.

"Goodness, you've gotten so tall!" she exclaimed. "How's your mom? How's Maisie? She must be so big too. "

I chatted with Mrs. O'Connell as we walked over to the rental car place.

"Thanks for coming to meet us, Jack and Maggie," my dad said to Kara's parents. "There really was no need, since we're renting a car."

"Ah, I said the same thing to Kara, but she wouldn't have missed meeting Miss Devin at the airport for all the world." I had almost forgotten that Mr. O'Connell was originally from Ireland, and had an accent. It was very musical-sounding.

"I had to greet Devin as soon as she stepped foot on

the East Coast," Kara stated. "Otherwise what kind of best friend would I be?"

"You know, Mike, you can always change your mind about the hotel and come be our guest instead," Mr. O'Connell offered.

"Thanks, Jack, but we don't want to intrude. Plus I've got some early-morning business meetings," my dad replied. "But Devin will be sleeping over Saturday night after the big party. That's all she's been talking about!"

"I've got some special plans for us tonight, too, Devin." Kara's big blue eyes sparkled.

I smiled. Kara and I used to have the most fun together. We would go see a movie and whisper lines that we made up for the characters. Sometimes people would shush us, but that just made us laugh really hard. Once, we were asked to leave by an usher! I was so embarrassed, I wanted to crawl under my chair. But Kara brought out my silly, playful side. Sometimes we would go to the mall and pretend we were from a different country, and we had this made-up language we would speak, and dare each other to order something from the food court or ask a question of a clerk in the store. We always had such goofy times together. I was exhausted from the flight, and the thought of some one-on-one time doing mindless, funny things with Kara perked me up.

"We're going to Patruno's Pizza, and all the gang is going to be there!" she exclaimed. "Mr. Burke, can you drop Devin off after you get checked into the hotel? I'm sure Devin wants to wash up after being on that long flight. I remember how I felt when I flew to California last fall; it was like a slug had crawled on my tongue and left a sticky trail of bad breath behind it!"

Everyone laughed, but I felt a little disappointed that it wasn't going to be just Devin-and-Kara time. I mean, I was really looking forward to seeing all of my old friends, but I was a little beat. Some quiet time with Kara sounded more my speed right about then. But I didn't want to waste a second of being in Connecticut, so I agreed.

A thought occurred to me. "But we don't have our luggage!" I reminded everyone. "I have nothing to change into, or even my toothbrush to deal with slug breath."

Mrs. O'Connell made a *tsk-tsk* sound. "You might as well come home with us now. I have a new toothbrush still in the package that you can have, and Kara can share some of her clothes."

"Yes, let's go!" Kara grabbed my arm and started pulling.

I waved helplessly at my dad.

"I'll pick you up tonight at Patruno's!" he called back.

As we drove through Milford, the Connecticut town where I used to live, I felt a pang of nostalgia wash over me. I missed this pretty town. It was the beginning of spring, and the trees that lined the streets were just getting their buds. Everything looked greener than it did in Kentville, where we were always under a drought warning and couldn't water our lawns or wash our cars. The grass around our house looked like straw. But here we passed houses with green lawns, some with brightly colored daffodils and tulips. The other thing I really liked about Milford was how old it was. There were houses that dated back to before the Revolutionary War, and there was this big one that had a wraparound porch lined with columns. The house was all white with black shutters. I used to dream about growing up and living in a house like that. Everything in Kentville was new and nice, but I missed the history of Milford.

We passed our old home, and I gasped.

"They painted it!" I said, my voice catching.

Our house used to be this pretty sky blue color with white trim. I'd loved living in a blue house, because it was one of the only ones in town, and it made me feel special. It's one of the reasons why I was so excited when I joined the soccer team in Kentville and found out their colors were blue and white.

The house was yellow now, which was pretty, but it didn't look like the home I remembered. That made me so sad.

Kara sighed. "I wanted to tell you, but I knew how much you loved your blue house, and I just couldn't bring myself to say anything."

After that I got into a funk I couldn't shake. It didn't help when none of Kara's clothes fit me.

"Where's the flood?" Kara asked when I tried on her pants, which were several inches too short. We had always been the same size before, but now my growth spurt had changed that. I had to stay in my sweatpants, but at least I was able to fit into one of her longer T-shirts, and she loaned me a sweater, too, in case the night got a little chilly.

As promised, Mrs. O'Connell produced a toothbrush, and I went into the bathroom to wash my face and use the deodorant I had borrowed from Kara. I did feel better, but it wasn't the same as having my own stuff. I hoped the suitcase would arrive by the next day, like my dad had said. Not having any of my own things made me feel even more like a stranger in my hometown.

When I got out of the bathroom and went back into Kara's room, I was surprised to see her seated in front of a lighted makeup mirror.

"I thought we were just going to Patruno's," I said as I watched Kara applying what seemed like more makeup than the makeup artist Tenshi had used on me when I'd done those modeling gigs.

"Yes, but everyone will be there and they will all be made up too," Kara said as she pouted in the mirror, before grabbing a tube of pink lipstick and running it over her lips.

"Oh, really?" My hand flew up to my cheek. I didn't have any makeup on.

"I can share mine with you," Kara said as she brushed eye shadow over her lids.

"You know that's never really been my thing," I said and I watched, fascinated, as she applied makeup like a professional. "I didn't know you were into all that either."

"At Sienna's first sleepover party, she had all this makeup for us to try," Kara said. "It was really fun—like creating art right on my face. So I started watching makeup tutorials, and they're amazing! I can change my look whenever I want."

With that, she shut off the makeup light and turned to me. Her face, which was always pretty, looked very glamorous, like a movie star, or Frida on the set of one of her commercials.

"Wow!" I said, speechless. It made Kara look so different, as if she were someone I didn't really know. "And your mom lets you wear it?"

"Well, there are some rules," Kara said. "I can only wear a little bit to school, but when I'm getting together with the Ruesters, she lets me put on more."

"The what now?" I asked, completely lost.

Kara laughed. "The Ruesters. We're all fans of Rue Ella, who has the best makeup tutorials on YouTube. She has more than a million subscribers! So we call ourselves the Ruesters, like the bird, but we spell it *R-u-e*, like she spells her name."

I let all of this sink in. I mean, I was glad that Kara was having fun and everything, but this was all news to me.

"You never told me about this before," I said, feeling a little hurt.

"Well, we always have so much catching up to do when we chat," Kara said with a shrug. "I guess I just never mentioned it. Besides, you like talking about soccer more, so maybe I thought you'd be a little bored with the whole makeup thing."

"Oh," I said, at a loss for words.

"Let's get going," Kara said, standing. "The Ruesters are waiting for us."

At least Patruno's Pizza hasn't changed, I thought when Mr. O'Connell dropped us off in front of the building, located in downtown Milford on Main Street, where there were rows of office buildings and shops. The red awning was the same, along with the plain, stucco exterior. My mom and dad always called it a "dive" and said the décor and menu hadn't changed since the 1950s. But it was the most popular pizza place in Milford, and everyone went there.

When we stepped inside, I was greeted by a swarm of girls I almost didn't recognize: Madison, Jolie, Bella, Kaitlyn, and Rachel. I had known them all since elementary school, when we'd started playing soccer together, but they looked so different. Had I been gone only a year?

"Devin!" Madison squealed. She used to have frizzy red hair and freckles. Now her hair was smooth and straightened, and I couldn't spot a freckle anywhere on her made-up face.

"Look at you! You got so tall!" Jolie exclaimed. She had always been the tiniest, and she still was, but the short hair I remembered her having was longer now and twisted into a fancy braid around the crown of her head. She looked so elegant and cool.

Bella, Kaitlyn, and Rachel agreed with Jolie, all standing next to me to measure their height compared to mine. I was the tallest. "The California sunshine helped you grow, and look at those blond highlights in your hair. I love it! Where did you get it done?" Rachel asked.

I laughed. "On the soccer field, by the best hair stylist in California: the sun!"

"I can see one thing that will never change about you, Devin, and that's soccer!" Bella said cheerfully. "I quit the team this year. I wanted to focus on cheerleading instead."

"Oh. Well, good for you—" I began to say, but Kara interrupted me.

"Hey, you've got to meet Sienna," she said, pulling over a girl who looked like she might be a professional model. She wore her dark brown hair pulled up into a perfect high bun on the top of her head. Her dark brown eyes were painted with smoky eye shadow, and she had thick black eyeliner that extended from the corners of her eyes like wings. Her eyebrows were thick and perfectly shaped. I remember Tenshi having to get rid of the tiny unibrow I had connecting my eyebrows. I never really paid that much attention to those kinds of things. I felt my hand creeping up to between my eyes, wondering if it had grown back.

A small smile played on Sienna's lips. "This is the Devin I've heard so much about? I've got to say, I'm a little surprised. I was expecting more LA glamour, but you're the no-makeup, sandal-wearing hipster type, right?"

I looked down at my feet, still in the flip-flops—not sandals—that I had put on so early that morning in California. The idea was to make it easy to pass through the security checkpoint at the airport, where you had to take off your shoes. I had real shoes, nice ones, packed for the trip. But they were in Albuquerque, with the rest of my stuff.

I felt a wave of self-consciousness wash over me, thinking of my possible unibrow, my ratty old flip-flops, and the fact that I didn't have on any makeup, except the gloss Kara had lent me because my lips were super dry after my being on a six-hour flight.

When I had left Connecticut, Jolie and Kaitlyn had still been playing with dolls. So much had changed, and I was starting to feel unsure of myself and how to act around my old friends. Then there was Kara's new friend, Sienna. I wasn't sure what to make of her at all.

"Oh, Devin's not a hipster. She's a serious athlete," Kara interjected. "Makeup and fashion aren't really her thing."

"There's nothing wrong with makeup. I actually did a little modeling recently," I said nervously, trying to establish some firm footing in these unchartered waters.

"Really?" Sienna arched one of her perfect eyebrows and looked at me in disbelief.

"Yeah, well . . . ," I started to mumble, feeling uneasy under Sienna's penetrating gaze, when Madison clapped her hands together.

"Come on, Ruesters. Let's get a table!"

Everyone grabbed a seat, and I wanted to sit next to Kara, but Sienna slid into the open spot next to her, so I settled for squeezing in between Madison and Rachel instead. They all pulled out their phones and started chatting about Rue Ella, pulling up photos of her latest makeovers on Instagram and playing her makeup tutorials on YouTube. I felt left out of the conversation, without much to add. It was not how I'd expected my reunion with Kara to go.

Back in California, Zoe was very into fashion and makeup, but we always talked about lots of other things, too. It seemed like the Ruesters were only interested in one topic, and it was one that I didn't really know anything about.

Once the pizza we ordered came, the topic changed to celebrities, and I felt relieved. That was one thing I could talk about.

"My friend Frida from California was in *Mall Mania*, the TV movie. She's also been in a bunch of commercials," I said, trying to finally be a part of the conversation.

"OMG, I love that movie," Jolie said. "Who did she play?"

"She was Cassidy, Brady McCoy's sister," I told them, a little bit proudly, I have to admit. I doubted that any of them knew a real-life movie star, including Sienna.

"Brady McCoy, the pop star?" Kaitlyn asked, her eyes wide. "She got to meet him? Awesome!"

I nodded. "Yes, and I met him too. Frida got him to

show up for a fund-raiser that our soccer team held. It was really cool. I never met any movie stars or famous singers when I lived here."

Kara frowned. "I guess Connecticut is just too basic for you now, huh?"

I was surprised. Kara, usually so smiley and easygoing, seemed mad at me.

"No, of course not—" I started, but before I could explain further, Sienna interrupted me.

"The basic one is Brady McCoy. He is SO over," she said, rolling her eyes. "Did you meet anyone else, Devin?"

All the Ruesters eyes locked on to me expectantly.

"Did you?" Jolie asked, her eyes hopeful.

I shook my head, and everyone looked disappointed as they picked up their phones again and returned to talking about fashion and celebrities. I tried to make eye contact with Kara to see if she was actually mad, but she wouldn't look at me.

When everyone's parents showed up to take them home, I headed out the door with the Ruesters. My dad was parked across the street, leaning against the rental car, a blue sedan. My heart leaped when I saw him. The night had been so confusing and weird. It was like a dream, where everything that felt like it should have been familiar was just slightly off. But my dad looked the same, and his smile reassured me. I once again felt on familiar ground.

Kara and Sienna walked past me, and I wanted to stop Kara to say good night, but then I started getting angry. I'd come all the way here from California, and Kara wasn't even going to say good-bye?

I was supposed to be spending the day with her the next day. Would Sienna tag along too?

Right then and there, I almost started to cry. Nothing was the way I had imagined it would be. I remembered how badly I'd wanted to go to Charlotte's party and to see Kara. I'd even used some of the money I'd earned from modeling to pay for part of my plane ticket. Now I had to wonder if I'd made a huge mistake!

CHAPTER FOUR

It was eight o'clock when we got to the hotel room, which meant five o'clock back in California, but I felt like I hadn't slept in days. Dad's company had put him in one of those hotels that have apartments in them, so I had my own little room to myself, and that was nice. I collapsed onto the bed, and Dad walked in carrying a plastic bag.

"The airline is sending our bags to the hotel tomorrow, but they might not get here before Kara and her parents pick you up in the morning. I called Mom, and she told me what to get you, so I picked up some things at the department store down the road. I had to get myself a suit jacket too," he said.

"Thanks!" I said.

I dumped the bag out onto my bed. There was some deodorant and a brand-new toothbrush. A package of underwear in my size. Socks and a pair of white sneakers. There was a T-shirt with a picture of the Eiffel Tower on it that said PARIS, and a pair of skinny jeans.

"Mom told you to get me a T-shirt with Paris on it?" I asked.

"No, she just gave me your sizes," he said. "I thought it was cool."

I gave him a hug. "It's great, Dad. Thanks. I'll be so glad when my real stuff gets here."

Then I took a shower, which felt amazing, and climbed into bed wearing the T-shirt Kara had lent me. There were a bunch of texts on my phone.

The first one was from Charlotte.

Devin! I heard you landed. Sorry I can't see you until the party, but I'm so busy! It's so cool that you're coming! Can't wait 2cu!

I replied: I am so excited!

The rest of the texts were from my Kicks friends.

From Emma: Did u land safely?

From Frida: How was the flight? Did you meet any celebrities in the airport?

From Zoe: Miss you, Dev!

From Jessi: Devin, we had tacos today in the caf. They almost made up for there being no you. ☹ 🌮 ☺

That one made me literally LOL. I decided to answer them all in a group text:

The plane ride was long! I wish I had tacos on the plane, Jessi. My luggage is lost. MY BEAUTIFUL DRESS is LOST!

Aaaargh! Went out 4 pizza with Kara and friends tonight. It wuz weird. Kara has a surprise trip planned for me tomorrow. Love you all and miss you. 😗

I knew my phone was going to start pinging with replies, so I turned it off and went to sleep. I was so tired!

In my dreams I saw an empty luggage conveyor belt spinning . . . and spinning . . . and spinning . . .

"Rise and shine, Devin!"

I slowly opened my eyes to see Dad in the doorway of my room, already showered and dressed.

"My meeting's at ten, and the O'Connells will be here at nine, which is about an hour from now," he informed me. "I've got breakfast if you want to eat with me."

"Yeah, okay," I mumbled groggily. I changed into my new clothes and stumbled into the kitchen.

"I popped into the bagel shop next door while you were sleeping," Dad said, and the smell of warm bagels hit my nose and made my stomach rumble.

"Everything with cream cheese?" I asked hopefully.

"Of course!" Dad said, and I sat at the kitchen island and gratefully unwrapped my bagel. Dad slid a container of orange juice at me.

I bit into the salty, oniony, garlicky bagel, crisp on the outside and chewy on the inside.

"They just don't make them like this in California," Dad said, and I nodded in agreement, because my mouth was full.

"This is awesome," I told him. "Thanks!" I sucked down some orange juice.

After that we ate our bagels in silence, because it's not easy to talk and eat bagels at the same time. When we were finished, Dad asked, "How are you doing? Recovered from the flight?"

"I think so," I answered.

"Did you have fun last night with your friends?" Dad asked.

I hesitated. Dad raised his eyebrows.

"What? No fun?" he asked.

I shrugged. "I think I was just tired. It's . . . not the same, exactly."

Dad nodded. "It's funny how life can change so quickly," he said. "I swore I would never get used to California, but when I went outside today, I thought it was weird that there were no palm trees."

I laughed. "Right? I guess we're really Californians now."

"If only they could solve the bagel problem," Dad said.

Talking with Dad, and eating that bagel, put me in a pretty good mood. While I waited for Kara and her parents, I checked my phone. As I had suspected, my friends had a lot to say about my group text.

Poor Devin! Emma texted.

If your surprise is a Broadway show, take pictures of the theater! Frida replied. **And I hope you get your luggage back!**

NOT THE DRESS! Zoe texted.

I could have told you CT was weird, Dev. 😜 was from Jessi.

Then I got a text from Kara that she and her parents were outside. I hugged Dad.

"I'll see you later," I said. "Good luck with your meeting."

"Thanks, Devin," he replied. "Have fun!"

I headed outside, where Kara was waiting for me. She hugged me.

"We have such an awesome day planned!" she said.

It felt just like the day before at the airport—there was no tension, and if Kara had been mad at me the night before, she wasn't now. I breathed a sigh of relief and started to get excited about the day.

"What are we doing?" I asked as Kara led me to the car.

Before Kara could answer, I climbed into the backseat and said hello to her mom and dad, who were in the front seats.

"Thanks so much for spending the day with me," I said.

"Have you told Devin our plans?" Mrs. O'Connell asked.

"I was just about to," Kara said. She looked at me. "*T. rex!*"

I gasped. "No way!"

Every year when Kara and I were growing up, our parents would take us to the American Museum of Natural History in Manhattan. There were lots of cool things to see, but our favorite were the dinosaurs. The museum had enormous skeletons! We'd both had a dinosaur obsession when we were, like, five. And even after we'd outgrown it, we'd always loved seeing the exhibit. I think I was eight or nine the last time we had gone there together.

"We'll do the museum first, and then have lunch, and if the weather stays nice, maybe we can head down to Times Square," Mrs. O'Connell said.

"That sounds awesome," I said. "Thank you!"

It took us more than an hour to ride into Manhattan, and there was lots of traffic, as always. I didn't mind because Kara and I talked the whole way, about all kinds of things— her boring history teacher, the Kicks making the playoffs, our favorite shows to watch online. Kara and I were back to normal again!

Mr. O'Connell drove through the busy streets, and I gazed up at the tall buildings and watched the hordes of people walking quickly on the sidewalks, almost all of them talking on their phones. Car horns blared, and images of celebrities glowed on digital billboards high in the sky.

"There's no place like Manhattan," I said.

"That's right," Kara agreed. "Maybe after high school, we could both go to college here. We could be roommates!"

"Maybe," I said, but then I wondered: How many schools in Manhattan had soccer teams? Was there any room for soccer fields in this city? I'd have to check that out. Of course, Jessi and I had talked about getting sports scholarships and going to college together at Stanford University, because they had an awesome women's soccer program. But I didn't mention that to Kara.

We pulled into the underground parking garage next to

the museum and then walked up to the entrance.

"Your dad and I are going to check out the new exhibit on oceans," Mrs. O'Connell said. "Do you want to come with us?"

I looked at Kara.

"We have to do the dinosaurs first," Kara said. "Is that okay?"

"Meet us at the café here at twelve thirty," Mr. O'Connell said. "And do not leave the museum!"

"Of course we won't," Kara promised. Then she grabbed my hand.

"Thank you again!" I called behind me as Kara and I raced to the dinosaur exhibit.

We stopped in our tracks at the sight of a massive dinosaur skeleton with a banner overhead that read THE TITANOSAUR. It had a really long neck and a giant head, and there was a long tail snaking behind it.

"Whoa," I said. "I don't remember this one."

"It's new," Kara told me, and we walked over to the display and read the description.

"It's one hundred and twenty-two feet long," I remarked, reading from the display.

"And more than a hundred million years old," Kara added. "Wow!"

We wandered through the exhibit, past glass cases holding giant dinosaur bones, and platforms with fossilized skeletons.

"Ooh, look. There's the duck-billed dinosaur!" Kara said,

and we walked over to it. "Remember when I asked the tour guide if it quacked?"

I smiled. "Remember when we played dinosaurs during recess at school?"

Kara nodded. "Ryan Zinski always had to be the *T. rex* and chase us all around the yard."

"He never caught us, though," I said.

"Nah, we were too fast," Kara said with a grin.

The memories of me and Kara when we were little were sweet, and kind of sad, too. Those days of being together every day at school were gone.

"What should we do next?" Kara asked.

"I wouldn't mind seeing that ocean exhibit," I told her.

We checked out the exhibit, and then the gift shop, where I impulsively bought a T-shirt with the Titanosaur on it for me and a stuffed dinosaur for Maisie. Then we met Kara's parents in the museum café.

"The rain is supposed to hold off until tonight," Mrs. O'Connell told us as we ate our sandwich wraps. "I think we should take the train down to Times Square for a bit. What do you think?"

"Yes!" Kara said. "There's an accessories shop there that Sienna says has the cutest earrings."

I remembered something. "There are Broadway theaters near Times Square, right?" I asked, and Kara's mom nodded. "I promised Frida that I would take some pictures for her. Maybe we could walk around there a little bit so I could shoot some of the signs?"

"Of course," Mrs. O'Connell said. "What a fun idea!"

I could have sworn I saw Kara roll her eyes, but I wasn't sure. *What's that about?* I wondered.

Soon we were browsing the accessories shop that Kara had mentioned. Sienna was right—the place had a lot of nice jewelry. I spotted this rack of adorable little beaded bracelets.

"This is perfect! I can get one for everybody in a different color," I said.

Kara raised an eyebrow. "By 'everybody' you mean . . ."

"Jessi, Emma, Zoe, and Frida," I said. "And I should get one for Sabine, too, for helping me get my dress."

Kara gave this big sigh.

"What's the matter?" I asked.

"I thought this visit was supposed to be about you and me," she said.

"It is," I told her. "What do you mean?"

"It's just . . . you keep talking about the Kicks, and now you're buying them presents, and then we have to go take pictures for your friend Frida . . ." Her voice trailed off.

I didn't know how to respond. Kara sounded jealous, which was crazy, because I had flown all the way across the country just to see her and go to Charlotte's party!

"I'm just . . . It's nice to bring stuff back for people when you go on a trip," I said. "And I talk about the Kicks because that's an important part of my life."

Mrs. O'Connell walked up to us. "Almost ready to check

out? We should take a walk down Broadway and then head home before rush hour starts."

"We don't have to do the Broadway thing," I said, trying to appease Kara.

"Of course we do! It'll be fun!" Kara's mom insisted, and this time I *definitely* saw Kara roll her eyes.

Kara and I paid for our purchases, and the four of us set out on a Broadway walk. We walked from Forty-Second Street to Forty-Eighth Street, and I snapped photos of every Broadway marquee I saw. I kept my eyes out for celebrities because I knew that would blow Frida's mind, but I didn't see any.

Then we hopped back onto the subway and returned to the parking garage. Even though we had beat rush hour, it still took us more than two hours to get back to Connecticut. And this time Kara and I didn't spend the ride talking. Kara put her headphones in as soon as we got into the car!

I hadn't brought my headphones with me, so I spent the ride texting my Broadway photos to Frida. She responded to each one.

Ooh, the Music Box Theatre! It's such a pretty theater, don't you think?

The Helen Hayes Theatre! Her career lasted 80 years. Can you imagine if I'm still acting when I'm 92?

Normally Frida's theater talk would bore me, but as I read her texts, I could almost imagine that she was in the car with us. She would have loved New York City!

When we got back to Connecticut, we met my Dad at a

Sarkey's Restaurant, a burger place where we always used to go when Kara and I were kids. Kara's bad mood had thawed out a little, and as we ate our burgers, we talked about all of the memories we had of being together at Sarkey's. When it came time for me to go back to the hotel, Kara gave me another big hug.

"We're picking you up in the morning for breakfast at the Pancake House," she told me. "And then you're coming to soccer practice with me."

"That sounds awesome," I said, and I meant it. I was so confused! It felt like our friendship was on a giant seesaw, and I didn't know whether we were up or down.

When we got back to the hotel, Dad asked, "How was your day?"

"Nice, but tiring," I said, and I looked around the room. "Hey, did our bags come?"

"No," Dad said. "Sorry, honey. I didn't want to spoil our dinner by telling you. Now the airline is saying our bags will be here tomorrow."

"They *have* to come tomorrow!" I said. "I can't go to Charlotte's party in skinny jeans and a Paris T-shirt!"

"We'll figure something out," Dad promised.

"Like what?" I said crossly. I knew it wasn't his fault, but I was starting to freak out.

Then Dad's phone rang. "It's your mom. Let me take this."

I went into my little room and flopped down onto the bed, my mind racing. What was I going to do without my dress? I sent another group text to my friends to update them.

Went to NYC today. Saw dinosaurs at the museum. Got back to hotel and my bag is still not here. WHAT AM I GOING TO DO WITHOUT MY DRESS?

I was not normally so dramatic, but it felt good to get it out. I knew my Kicks friends would understand.

I got up and went into the kitchen to get some water. That's when I heard my dad talking on the phone.

". . . good opportunity, honey, but relocating back here? We're just getting used to California."

I froze.

Relocating?

Back *here*?

Was that what Dad's big business trip was all about—us moving back to Connecticut?

A few months before, I might have been thrilled to get this news. When we had left Connecticut, I was so sad. I dreamed that we'd come back someday. But now?

Before I could process what I'd just heard, my phone started pinging with texts.

Don't panic, Devin!

We'll help you.

Dinosaurs are awesome!

I laughed, and then I got sad again. Did I really want to leave Jessi, Emma, Zoe, and Frida behind? Would I be happy if I wasn't playing for the Kicks anymore?

I was pretty sure I knew what the answer was, and my heart sank.

I didn't want to move back to Connecticut!

CHAPTER five

The smell of a crisp spring morning on a soccer field in Connecticut made me feel the most at home since the plane had first touched down. This was familiar territory, and at least there was one thing I could count on: the game of soccer had not changed while I was away in California!

But Kara had. And maybe I had too. What would it mean to move back?

I breathed in the fresh air, the smell of earthy, woodsy grass filling my nose. The field sparkled with dew, something that I didn't see much in dry California. Feeling chilly, I wrapped my arms around myself. I was still wearing the Paris T-shirt, and wishing I had the hoodie that was packed in my suitcase.

When Kara and I got to the field, the other girls were milling around, talking.

"Hey, I need to ask Jolie something," Kara said. "One sec."

She jogged off, and I stood there, watching my old friends talking and laughing as they stretched and got ready for practice. Then Sienna walked up to me. I quickly looked around. There was no way to avoid her. What did she want?

"How you doing, LA?" she asked, and it sounded like an insult, the way someone would say, "Way to go, genius" after you did something really dumb.

I flashed back to the comment she had made the other night, that I wasn't as glamorous as she had expected. I did a mental eye roll. I didn't even live in Los Angeles. I lived in Kentville, and while it was nice, no one would call it glamorous!

"Fine," I said.

"You don't look fine," Sienna said. "You seem sad."

Wait, was Sienna actually being nice to me?

"I'm just tired," I said.

"I guess it must be hard being away from your friends," she said.

I shrugged. "Sure." Where was this going?

Then the team's coach, Coach Bailey, walked out onto the field, and all of the players jogged toward her. Kara had told me that Coach Bailey was also her math teacher, and Kara really liked her.

Kara stopped in front of me on her way toward the coach. "I guess you can hang out on the bench while we practice."

I nodded. "That's fine. I'll be jealous watching all of you play, though."

Kara's eyes lit up. "Why don't we ask Coach if you can join the practice?"

Kara grabbed my hand and pulled me up to Coach Bailey.

"Coach, this is my friend Devin. She was on the Cosmos last year, and she's visiting this weekend. Can she practice with us?" Kara asked.

"Devin Burke?" Coach asked.

I nodded.

She smiled. "Coach Peterson mentioned you. She said you were one of her best players. You're welcome to join us for practice."

"Thanks!" I said. I looked down at my feet. "I don't have cleats with me. Just sneakers. Is that okay?"

"That should be fine," she said, and then she turned to the other girls and clapped her hands. "Okay. Let's get practice started. Give me some laps!"

We started jogging around the track. It felt good to be moving, and I was grateful that Coach Bailey had let me join in. I jogged past Madison, Rachel, Kaitlin, and Jolie.

"Slow down, Devin! You're making us look bad," Rachel joked.

Even though I knew she was kidding, I slowed down a little bit.

"Sorry," I said. "I guess I just like doing laps."

Kara caught up to me. "Same old Devin," she said. "Always leaving us in the dust."

It was supposed to be a compliment—I think—but I

thought I heard a little bit of annoyance in Kara's voice. So I just kept moving forward, and focused on the blue sky and the cool air on my face, until Coach blew her whistle. The team lined up in front of her, and I joined them, ending up between Kara and Madison.

"Let's do some high knees, up to the line, then backward until you get back to start," Coach instructed.

We launched into the activity. I knew it was a good way to activate the muscles in the legs and hips, because Coach Flores had us do this a lot.

Next Coach Bailey had us do butt kicks, which was another slow jog, but you did this exercise while bringing your feet as close to your butt as you possibly could, to strengthen your hamstrings. We did it both forward and backward before we launched into lunges.

A few times Kara looked over at me and flashed that big smile I knew and loved, making me think that things were going to be okay with us. After all, it had been a while since we had seen each other. Maybe the seesaw feelings I was having were totally normal after spending time apart and would stop soon. I hoped so, especially if what my dad had said on the phone last night about relocating was true.

If that did happen, I'd have a lot of friends to come back to, and they were all great in so many ways. Madison was really funny, Jolie had a great imagination, Kaitlin adored animals, and Rachel was supersmart and a good writer. She used to help us all with our homework writing assignments. But then I felt a tug at my heart. I knew that while they'd always be my friends, none of them could replace Emma and her kindness, Frida and her over-the-top dramatics, Zoe and her eye for style, and the fun factor that Jessi brought to everything she did.

I got lost in my thoughts as Coach Bailey divided the girls up into two teams for a scrimmage. I ended up on a team with Kara, Madison, and eight other girls I didn't know. One of them, a girl with curly brown hair, nodded at me.

"Are you really as good as Coach Peterson says you are?" she asked.

I blushed, not sure how to answer.

Kara answered for me. "She is, Fabiola. Don't worry. You're going to be glad she's on our team."

Fabiola smiled. "Let's see what you got, then, Cali girl."

"Thanks," I whispered to Kara. And then my heart started to beat quickly. Now I had something to prove!

Sienna was on the other team, along with Jolie and Rachel. I saw Sienna whispering something into Jolie's ear. Jolie looked up at me and then turned back to Sienna and shook her head.

I wondered what that was about, but I didn't have time to think about it as we got into a three-four-three formation (three defenders, four midfielders, three forwards). Coach Bailey put Kara and me in as forwards.

Fabiola, a midfielder, intercepted a pass from the other team and sent it to me, with enough power behind her kick that I had to run like crazy to keep up with the ball. Once I was on it, I kept it close. The defenders ran to stop me, but luckily I had a clear shot to Kara. I passed her the ball, and she got it, charged toward Rachel at the goal, and shot it right past her into the net.

"Woo-hoo!" Kara yelled. "We still got our soccer mojo, Devin!"

I ran up to her and we hugged.

The scrimmage played on, and we got control of the ball again. Fabiola kicked it deep into the opponent's side, and Kara and I ran toward the goal. Sienna was dribbling the ball, and I shot up to her like a streak of lightning and kicked it away from her.

I charged toward the goal but got blocked by a defender. I turned my back on her and dribbled the ball to the side, a trick I had learned during the winter league while I was on the Griffons team. When I got clear, I raced down the field, my heart pounding. I had a clear shot of the goal, when out of nowhere I felt something slam into my side.

I lost my balance and stumbled, and the ball got away from me. I clutched my side. That had hurt.

I felt like the wind had been knocked out of me, and I doubled over for a second, trying to catch my breath. When I looked up, I saw Sienna kicking the ball down the field, away from the goal. I heard a whistle blowing, and then Coach Bailey saying sternly, "That was way too rough, Sienna. What were you thinking?"

I stood up, not letting it slow me down.

"No problem. I'm good to go!" I called out. I wanted to play, and now that I had the goal in my sights, I wasn't going to stop until I scored.

We resumed the scrimmage, and working together

with Kara, I was able to solidly pack a goal into the net. It felt great.

I managed to score twice more during the scrimmage, which was a short one—two periods, ten minutes each. When Coach Bailey's whistle blew, our team had beaten Sienna's team by two points.

Fabiola high-fived me. "Great game, California!"

I grinned and high-fived her back. "Thanks!" Nearby I could see Sienna scowling, and I ignored her.

As we headed off the field, I heard a voice calling, "Devin! Devin!"

I broke off from the others as a tall girl with long red hair came running toward me and Kara excitedly.

"Charlotte!" I gasped. "Happy birthday!"

She hugged me first, and as she pulled away, she said, "I can't believe how much taller you are!"

"I've been hearing that a lot," I told her. "It's so cool you stopped by."

"Yeah, you must be crazy getting ready for the party," Kara said.

Charlotte was dressed casually in yoga pants, a T-shirt, a hoodie, and flip-flops.

"I'm on my way to a mani-pedi," she said. "We were passing by here, so I had to stop. Then my mom, sister, and I are going to lunch before I get my hair and makeup done. I'm so excited! I feel like a movie star or something."

"I'm sure you're going to look like one," Kara said.

"You're so sweet, Kara!" Charlotte said. "It's cool seeing you play. You both have gotten really good."

"Thanks," Kara said.

"You were a great teacher," I added.

"Those days were a lot of fun," Charlotte said. Then she turned to me. "Devin, you've got some amazing moves. Kara told me you're thinking of going pro someday?"

I shrugged. "I mean, it seems like an impossible dream, but I think I want to go for it," I answered.

"Then California is a good place to be," she said. "There are a lot of great colleges for soccer in California. It could start you off toward professional play."

"Yeah," I said, and then I glanced over at Kara. "But you know, there are colleges everywhere, right?"

"Just find one with a great soccer program," Charlotte said.

I nodded. "I promise."

"Good. You should go for it, Devin," she said. "Anyway, I've got to run. I'll see you tonight!"

Charlotte jogged away, and Kara turned to me.

"It was really nice of Charlotte to stop by," Kara said. "It makes me think of all the time we spent with her on the field, when we were just kids. We haven't lost that magic on the field, right, Devin?" she said, hanging an arm over my shoulder.

I smiled. "Nope, we haven't. Although, I did lose a little fairy dust when Sienna came crashing into me."

I didn't know it, but Sienna had walked up behind us and heard us.

"What's the matter, Devin, can't take it on the field?" she asked.

ALEX MORGAN

I really did not understand what her problem was with me. If I'd thought I had been imagining it before, after this last comment I now really believed that Sienna just didn't like me.

"I sure can, and if I remember correctly, I beat you in the process too, right?" I asked, a hand on my hip. Getting back on the field—and seeing Charlotte—had grounded me and made me remember who I was: a confident girl who was good at what she did, no matter what state she happened to be in, California or Connecticut.

"Whatever," Sienna said before she sauntered off.

Kara shook her head, clearly annoyed. "I don't see why you two can't get along."

"I haven't done anything," I protested, my feelings hurt. Hadn't Kara noticed that Sienna was the one who'd been saying snarky things to me from the moment we'd first met? And that she'd nearly creamed me on the soccer field today?

But then Kara's familiar, bright smile returned. "Hey, we've got the sweet sixteen party tonight to look forward to. We're going to have a blast!"

Once again, Kara and I were on the friendship seesaw. This was so confusing. But if Kara was looking forward to the party, I was too. Now all I had to do was hope and pray that my dress would be waiting for me back at the hotel!

CHAPTER SIX

"Please, please let our luggage be here," I whispered under my breath as my dad and I walked into the hotel lobby after soccer practice. I was also crossing my fingers.

Dad approached the reception desk and smiled at the woman standing there. "I'm hoping you've got some good news for us, Laura," he said.

"Hello, Mr. Burke." She typed on the computer screen in front of her before frowning. "I'm sorry, but your luggage has not arrived."

"Ugh!" I smacked the palm of my hand against my forehead. No dress. No party. I'd flown all the way out here just to be snarked at by Sienna. This was definitely *not* a trip to remember.

While I was having my mini meltdown, Laura continued to type.

"However, you did get a delivery," she said. "Actually,

not you, Mr. Burke, but a package came for Devin."

"A package? I'm not expecting anything." I said, surprised. Unless Sienna had sent me a box of snakes or something, I couldn't imagine what it was.

Laura retrieved a large white gift box from under the desk. It had a blue ribbon and a matching bow attached. She squinted at the gift tag.

"It says 'To Devin, from the Kicks,'" she read. "The Kicks. Is that some kind of dance group, like the Rockettes?"

I laughed. The Rockettes were a dance company that dressed all in the same outfits and did synchronized moves. Our family watched them every year during their television holiday special. I couldn't wait to tell that one to Jessi, Emma, Zoe, and Frida. I just imagined what our new team cheer would look like—lined up in a row, high-kicking!

"No, that's my soccer team," I said as I grabbed the box. "And I think they just saved the day for me!"

When my dad and I got into our hotel room, I put the big box on my bed and slid the ribbon off. Nestled inside the box, under sheets of tissue paper, was a royal blue dress. I carefully folded the paper back and pulled it out, holding my breath a little. Then I quickly tried it on.

The dress had a high neckline framed with cap sleeves over the fitted bodice. It came with a metallic silver belt that I put around my waist. The skirt had fluttering pleats and flared out with a crinoline lining, which made it poof around me. It hit about midthigh, which was a little shorter than my other dress, but I loved it. I spun around, and the skirt twirled like a dancer's. Maybe "Rockette" was fitting!

Also in the box was a metallic headband that matched the belt, and silver, sparkly high heels.

I grabbed my phone and took a mirror selfie before sending it in a group chat to the Kicks.

I 🤍 you all so much! You saved my life! How did you do it? Thank you!!!!!

My phone immediately got flooded with replies.

My cousin works with a designer in NYC. I told her what you like, and your size, and she picked it out and overnighted it to you. She gave it to us at a big discount, but we all chipped in! This was from Zoe.

You're welcome. Save it for my next red carpet premiere! Frida texted.

We'd never leave you stranded without a dress! Be safe in those heels—don't pull a me and trip! I laughed at Emma's text. She'd had to practice in heels for weeks before Zoe's bat mitzvah.

I told everyone it had to be blue so you wouldn't forget us. Have fun! Jessi replied.

I was interrupted in the Kicks text fest by a knock on my bedroom door.

"Devin, does it fit?" Dad called.

I opened the door. "See for yourself." I did another little twirl.

My dad smiled. "Devin, you look beautiful! And so grown-up. Being back in Milford has reminded me of when you were just a baby. Where did the time go?"

This was very sweet, but I didn't have time to deal with Dad's nostalgia. I had a party to get ready for!

I put the dress away in the box, and Dad dropped me off at Kara's so we could get ready together. I had the box tucked under my arm. Kara grabbed it as soon as she saw me.

"Let me see!" she said eagerly.

"It's not the same dress that I showed you," I told her as she pulled it out of the box. "Our luggage still hasn't come, so my friends bought me a dress."

Kara froze, looking at the dress in her hands. "They *bought* this for you?"

"Yes. Well, Zoe has a cousin who's a designer, and she—"

"*Of course* she does," Kara said, rolling her eyes. She let go of the dress.

Why is she acting like this? I wondered. I changed the subject.

"So, what are you wearing?" I asked. I looked around the room nervously. Was Sienna coming here to get ready too? I'd never even asked if she was going to the party, because it seemed like a sore subject between me and Kara.

"Sienna helped me pick my dress out, and I love it," she said as she walked over to her closet. "She was a little mad that Charlotte didn't invite her, but they only just met this year, and it's not like we're all in the same grade or anything."

"Sienna seems like she can get mad easily." The words just popped out of my mouth. But I wasn't lying.

Kara made a *tsk* noise with her tongue. "I thought you two would hit it off. I'm so confused about why you seemed not to like Sienna from the start."

"It wasn't me. It was her—" I started, and then stopped. "Look, Kara, maybe we should just not talk about Sienna, at least for tonight. I've been waiting for weeks to come here and go with you to Charlotte's party. Let's just try to forget it and have fun."

Kara hesitated, but then her big smile returned. "Okay, but only if you let me do your makeup!"

I dutifully sat in front of Kara's lighted makeup mirror as she used brushes and wands, and applied powder all over my face.

"Open your eyes now!" Kara said when she had finished.

I opened my eyes and gasped. Was that me, or one of Frida's movie star friends? My eyes had glittery shadow and were lined with kohl black liner, giving me a dramatic look. My cheekbones looked like a model's, and my lips were pouty and perfect. I'd had my makeup done by a professional when I'd modeled, but that had been for a natural look. This was full-on glam.

"Did you really learn how to do this from watching videos?" I said, shocked. "This is amazing!"

"I think I might be a makeup artist one day," Kara said. "I know we're not supposed to talk about her, but Sienna thinks I'm good enough."

"You could be if you wanted to." I was impressed. "I feel beautiful!"

"Now let me get mine on while you do your hair," Kara suggested.

I followed the instructions Zoe had texted me for my hair. I borrowed Kara's flat iron to straighten it, then used a tiny bit of gel to smooth it back and pull it into a long, high ponytail. I then added the silver, sparkly headband that had come with the dress. Simple and elegant.

By the time Kara was done, we both looked like superstars or maybe even top models. I was really surprised at the transformation, and I also wondered if Sienna was the one who had given Kara the idea to become a makeup artist, and why Kara had never mentioned it before.

We stood in front of the mirror together, admiring ourselves and each other. Kara's dress was supercute: a sleeveless, V-neck black dress with multicolored flowers embroidered all over it. The glossy tulle skirt flared out right above her knees, making it look like a ballerina's tutu. To complete the look, she wore strappy, high-heeled black sandals.

"This calls for a besties selfie!" she cried, and we took turns taking photos of ourselves together.

I felt a bit like Cinderella as Mr. O'Connell drove us to the event hall at the country club where Charlotte's party was being held.

The hall had many round tables scattered around a dance floor. Charlotte's colors were pink and white, and white linens covered all the tables, which were adorned with bouquets of pink and white flowers.

"I thought she was doing a World Cup theme?" I asked, remembering some images Charlotte had posted on social media a few weeks before.

"It was a toss-up between that theme and *Pretty in Pink*, and pink won," Kara said. "Not everything has to be about soccer, you know."

"I'm not complaining!" I promised. "This is really nice."

We picked up a pink table number card and found out that we were seated with Rachel, Madison, Jolie, Bella, and Kaitlyn. I secretly thought that this would be a lot more fun than Patruno's, since Sienna wasn't here to be all snarkmaster with me.

"Devin, you look gorgeous!" Rachel cried. "Kara must have done your makeup. She's the best out of all of us."

Kara smiled. "Thanks. You're sweet!"

I glanced around at my friends, who looked so glamorous. "You all did a great job yourselves!"

Jolie giggled. "Remember when we were little and walked around with skinned knees all the time?"

I got a little self-conscious. I had skinned my knees good wiping out at soccer practice earlier that week. They had mostly healed up, but I hoped no one noticed. I should have asked Kara to throw some makeup onto my knees, too!

Soon I didn't have time to worry about anything. Charlotte made her entrance in a gorgeous, light-pink ball gown that touched the floor. Her red hair was swept up into big, beautiful curls, with a tiara nestled in it.

"She really does look like Princess Ariel," I whispered to Kara. Because of her red hair, we always used to call her the Little Mermaid when we were younger.

Then the music started, and we all hit the dance floor. Kara and I clowned around together, coming up with crazy dance moves and making each other laugh. The friendship seesaw was definitely back on top, and I was happy.

Kara and I were dancing when Charlotte ran up to us and grabbed each of us by the hand. Then we all started twirling around.

"This is a great party!" I shouted over the music. "It's everything I dreamed about back in California!"

"It's so nice that you flew out here to celebrate with me, Devin," Charlotte said. "I hope we can talk before you leave. I want to hear all about California."

I nodded. "Definitely!"

The song ended, and Charlotte broke away from us. I ran back to our table to get a drink of water, a little sweaty and out of breath. When I checked my phone, there was a text from Jessi.

Baby is on the way! I'll keep you posted. Hurry home so you can meet the new little Duke!

I texted back emojis and then started asking questions. What hospital were they at? Was Jessi there with her parents or at home? How long had her mom been in labor for? Was it scary? I promised to go see her as soon as I got home, and we kept texting back and forth. I forgot about the dancing and the party for a while, until Kara came over.

"Devin! What are you doing?" She sounded annoyed.

"Um, I'm texting my friend Jessi—" I began, but before I could finish, Kara cut me off.

Kara rolled her eyes. "Seriously? Don't you, like, see Jessi every day? I never get to see you!" she said, her cheeks red and flushed from dancing.

"Yeah, but she's having a baby—I mean, her mom is having a baby." I got nervous, and the words wouldn't come out right.

"Whatever. I'm going to dance with my *friends*," she said, and then she stomped off in her high heels.

I sighed as I slumped in my chair. The friendship seesaw had just landed on the ground with a *thump*, and I think I had been knocked off!

CHAPTER SEVEN

The rest of the night was awkward.

Kara barely talked to me. She stayed glued to Madison and Jolie, and when we were all out on the dance floor, she never even looked at me!

The more I thought about what was happening, the angrier I got with Kara. She was being so unreasonable! I mean, I wasn't texting Jessi for no reason. Her mom was having a baby!

I was so upset that I stayed off the dance floor after that. I ate my dinner, but I didn't bother to hit the dessert table, which was full of pink cookies, pink cupcakes, and jars filled with pink candy. I thought about asking my dad to come pick me up, but I didn't. I had begged and begged to come to Connecticut for this party. He'd be upset if I asked him if I could go home in the middle of it! So I stuck it out.

Near the end of the party, the deejay asked everybody to come onto the dance floor for Charlotte's favorite song. I stayed at my table, even though Rachel tried to pull me away to dance with everybody. I was done, checked out, and did not feel like dancing.

After the song ended, Charlotte came over and sat down next to me.

"Is everything okay, Devin?" she asked.

"I'm fine," I said, and I suddenly felt bad. This was Charlotte's special party, and here she was, worried about me.

Charlotte didn't press me to find out what was wrong. "So, what's it like living in the land of sunshine all the time? I'm thinking of going to school out there. I really hate the winters here, you know?"

"I like winter, but yeah, the weather is basically always sunny, and you can be outdoors all the time without wearing sixteen layers of clothing," I replied, smiling for the first time in an hour.

"I guess you made some friends out there too?" she asked.

"I did," I answered. Then I found myself just blurting out everything that had happened. "I mean, that's normal, right? Only, Kara's acting like it's wrong that I have other friends besides her, which is just not fair. My friend Jessi texted me because her mom is having a baby, and I'm excited for her, and it's not like I was ignoring Kara, and . . ." I stopped. "Sorry. I'm not making any sense."

"It's okay," Charlotte said. "I fight with my friends sometimes too. But we usually work it out. That's just part of being friends."

"Thanks," I said, and I grinned. "Wow, I guess turning sixteen makes you super wise and smart, right?"

"Definitely not," Charlotte said. Then she jumped up and held out her hands. "Come on, Devin. This is my party, and I say you have to get back onto the dance floor. And you have to obey the birthday girl."

I giggled. "Yes, Your Highness!"

I followed her out to the dance floor, and even though Charlotte quickly got pulled away, I stayed. I found Rachel and Bella, and I danced with my old friends, including Kara, although it was awkward.

When the party ended, Kara's mom picked us up.

"So how was the party?" she asked.

"Okay," Kara replied, looking out the window.

"It was nice," I said.

"You girls seem quiet," her mom said. "You must be pooped from all that dancing!"

"Mmm-hmm," Kara replied, and she stared out the window.

Kara didn't talk to me the whole way to her house. When we got there, she and I headed upstairs to her room.

"You can shower first," she offered.

"Thanks," I said, and soon I felt clean and a little more awake and comfortable in sweats and a T-shirt. Her dad had set up a small cot for me in Kara's room, with a sleeping bag and pillows, and I stretched out on top of it, waiting for Kara to finish her shower.

Kara finally came out in her pajamas, drying her hair with a towel. She tossed the towel over her desk chair and climbed into her bed. Then she picked up her phone and started scrolling.

Is she ignoring me? I wondered. I remembered what Charlotte had said about friends working things out, so I decided to give it a try.

"Kara, you're acting like you're mad at me," I said.

Kara didn't answer. She didn't take her eyes off her phone.

I sat up. "Okay, this proves you're *definitely* mad at me. What's your problem?"

Kara lowered her phone. "You know what my problem is, Devin. I already told you, but you don't seem to care. You came all the way out here to Connecticut, and you're ignoring me because of your friends in California."

"Jessi's mom is having a *baby*," I said. "That's a big deal. And it's not like I was texting her all night. It was just, like, a minute."

"Why were you even texting your friends at the party?" Kara shot back.

"*She* texted *me*," I countered. "And anyway, everybody had their phones out."

"Whatever," Kara replied.

"Do not 'whatever' me!" I said, and I heard my voice getting loud, but I couldn't stop. "I could say the same thing about you ignoring me. My first night here, we had to do something with Sienna and your friends. You didn't even—"

"Ha!" Kara said. "Sienna said you would blame it on her. She says you're jealous of our friendship. And you're trying to make me feel jealous with Jessi. She also said—"

"I don't care what Sienna said!" I was yelling now. "I do not care at all!"

Mrs. O'Connell knocked on the door. "Girls, is everything okay?"

My heart was pounding and my blood was boiling. I didn't answer Kara's mom, but I picked up my phone. I texted my dad.

Can you come get me? Please?

"Girls?" Mrs. O'Connell stepped into the room.

Is everything okay? Dad asked.

Just please come get me.

Be there in ten.

"Kara, what's going on?" her mom asked.

"Ask Devin. She's the one with the problem," Kara replied.

"I'm sorry, Mrs. O'Connell," I said. "My dad is coming to get me. I'm just—I need to go."

Mrs. O'Connell looked from me to Kara, and I'm pretty sure she figured out what was happening.

"Are you sure you don't want to stay, Devin? You're flying out tomorrow," she said.

I looked at Kara, waiting for her to say something. To

say she was sorry. To beg me to stay. But she didn't say anything.

"I'm sure," I said.

Then I got all my stuff together and left Kara without another word. Dad came to the door a few minutes later. I hugged Kara's mom, thanked her, and when I got into the car, I broke down sobbing.

"Fight with Kara?" Dad asked.

I nodded, still crying.

"Must have been a pretty bad one," he said. "Do you want to talk about it?"

I shook my head. "Not right now," I croaked, my voice hoarse from crying. "Is that okay?"

"I'm here when you're ready," Dad said. "Now let's get back to the hotel. We've got to be up fairly early for our flight tomorrow."

I nodded, grateful that Dad hadn't pushed me to talk and wasn't pummeling me with questions.

I was so exhausted that I slept soundly that night. I groaned when the alarm went off at six the next morning, but I quickly got out of bed. Before the day was over, I would be back in California. That made me happy, but I felt sad at the same time. It was awful to be leaving things with Kara like this. It wasn't how I wanted to say good-bye!

I showered and packed, and just as we were about to leave, a valet came up to our room with our suitcases!

My dad simply looked at them and sighed. "Now we can put them right back on the plane."

"Maybe I should wear my first dress to the airport, so I can finally get a chance to show it off," I joked.

"You can wear whatever you like, but I bet you'll be more comfortable in sweats and a T-shirt," Dad said.

"Good point," I said, and quickly put on a fresh outfit from my suitcase, just before our ride to the airport came.

The flight back home was basically the same as the one to Connecticut—long and unexciting. I didn't sleep on the plane. Dad asked if I wanted to watch a movie with him in the seats, and we ended up watching two long superhero films back-to-back.

We landed in California at two o'clock, and then it took us two hours to get home from the airport. It was four o'clock when we walked through the front door, but to me it felt like seven o'clock, the time back in Connecticut.

"I made some chicken and rice," Mom said after she hugged both me and Dad. "I figured you'd be hungry now, being on East Coast time."

"Yes!" I said, and sat down at the table. I inhaled the dinner Mom had made for us, down to the last shred of lettuce in the salad. Mom and Maisie had a lot of questions about the party, and I told them everything (except the part about me and Kara fighting).

Maisie was being really sweet to me, like she had forgotten all about our fight before I'd left—where she'd said she wouldn't miss me. I had already forgiven her, because we said stuff like that to each other all the time. I think it was because we were sisters, and we spent so much time together that we got on each other's nerves. But we really do love each other.

"How big exactly was that new dinosaur at the museum?" she asked.

"Soooo big," I told her. "It had a very, very long neck."

"As long as a school bus?" she asked.

"Longer, I think," I replied, and her eyes got wide.

That reminded me of something. I went to my bag and took out the stuffed dinosaur I'd gotten for Maisie and handed it to her.

"A *T. rex*!" she cried happily. "My favorite!"

"I know," I said. "I must have read you that *Timmy the T-Rex* book a million times when you were six. Remember?"

Maisie just beamed at me, and I saw Mom and Dad exchange a look—you know, that look parents give each other when they're happy with their kids.

I yawned. "I think I might take a nap," I said.

"Do whatever you need to do to be fresh for school tomorrow," Mom advised.

I brought my luggage upstairs and stretched out on my bed. It felt so comfy and familiar, not like the hotel bed. I closed my eyes and drifted off to sleep with the California sunshine streaming through my window.

The sound of my phone vibrating startled me out of my nap. Groggy, I picked it up and blinked, staring at a barrage of texts from Jessi. First there were photos of an adorable baby boy with tiny clutched fists and closed eyes, wrapped in a blue blanket. Then there were a bunch of frantic messages.

Are u back yet?

Come 2 the hospital!

Where are u?

I groaned. I had promised Jessi I would go see her as soon as I got home! But I was so beat—I couldn't imagine going anywhere.

Sorry. I am soooooo tired, I typed. See you soon?

Whatever, Jessi typed back.

Uh-oh, I thought. Last night I'd gotten a "whatever" from Kara, and now one from Jessi. I couldn't deal with two best friends being angry with me, so I called Jessi.

"I'm not supposed to talk on the phone in the hospital," she said.

"Jessi, I am so happy for your new little brother, and I can't wait to meet him," I said quickly. "But I am really tired. I'm still on East Coast time. I'll see if my mom can bring me tomorrow."

"Tomorrow we have practice," Jessi said.

I frowned. "Okay. Tuesday, then."

"Fine," Jessi said, and hung up on me. I could tell that she was upset.

I put down the phone. Now Jessi was mad at me too?

I stretched and climbed out of bed, thinking a cookie would help my mood. Mom and Dad were at the kitchen table, whispering. They stopped abruptly when I walked in.

"Devin, I thought you were sleeping," Mom said.

"Jessi woke me up with a text," I said, grabbing a box of cookies from the closet. (And by "cookies," I meant round things made of oats and dried fruit, the kind of thing that passes for a cookie in my Mom's ultra-healthy kitchen.) "Mom, can we go see Jessi's new baby brother on Tuesday?"

"Of course," Mom replied. "Mrs. Dukes will probably be back from the hospital by then. I'll make them a quinoa casserole."

"That would be nice," I said, and I took two cookies and headed back upstairs.

What were Mom and Dad whispering about? I wondered. They were probably talking about moving back to Connecticut for Dad's job, I guessed.

I bit into my cookie, examining my feelings about this. I thought I belonged in California now, but did I? I was starting to think I didn't belong *anywhere*, and that was a feeling not even a cookie could wash away.

CHAPTER EIGHT

"Deeeeeeeviiiiiiiiiiiiiiiiiiin!"

Jessi ran up to me the next morning in the school hallway and crushed me in a hug.

"Whoa!" I said, laughing as her forceful hug pushed us into my locker.

"I missed you so much!" she cried.

"I missed you too!" I said. "I'm relieved. I thought you were mad at me."

"I was, but my emotions are all over the place," Jessi said. "It took Mom, like, almost twenty-four hours to have Oliver, and—"

"His name is Oliver? That's such a cute name!" I shrieked.

"He's the cutest thing ever!" Jessi agreed. "Anyway, I know you were tired yesterday, and that's cool. I'm exhausted too, and I'm just so excited about this kid. He's such a little nugget!"

"He *is* a little nugget," I agreed. "Do you have more pictures?"

"Yes, tons!" She pulled her phone out to show me just as the bell rang. "Darn it! Get ready for the nugget photo spectacular at lunch."

"I can't wait!" I said as I hurried off to class, happy that Jessi wasn't mad. I was thinking of lunch, being surrounded by my friends, when a pang of worry hit me. What would happen if I moved back to Connecticut? Would I have to eat lunch with Kara and Sienna every day and keep going up and down on that friendship seesaw? Or would I have no friends at all, and have to eat by myself? I shuddered and shook my head.

The issue was still on my mind at lunch as Jessi, Frida, Emma, Zoe, and I gathered at our usual table in the cafeteria.

"Devin! You're back!" Emma squealed, and I got wrapped in another bear hug, which soon became a hug sandwich as Frida, Zoe, and Jessi joined in.

"Wow. It's like I've been gone for a month!" I joked, feeling a little overwhelmed at all the attention, but also happy. They'd missed me. They'd really missed me!

"We're so glad you're home. We can't help it!" Emma hugged me tighter.

"I've got the best friends ever," I said. "I can't believe that you sent me the most beautiful dress in the world for the party."

"We'd never let you down, Devin," Zoe said solemnly. "Especially when it comes to fashion."

Zoe looked as fashionable as always, wearing a super-cute black-and-white checkered dress, paired with a denim jacket and high-top sneakers. Her hair was pulled back into a tiny ponytail at the nape of her neck.

"I've only been away a few days, and your hair is long enough for a ponytail already!" I exclaimed. "How did that happen?"

"It's growing really fast," Zoe said.

"Pretty soon it'll be down to your ankles," Emma remarked. She was wearing her usual outfit: a pair of jeans and a T-shirt. This shirt had big, graphic rainbow-colored letters spelling out GOOD VIBES. That was Emma, all right. Sharing positive, good vibes with everyone she met.

Frida's reddish-brown hair was pulled into a braid down the left side of her head, not a look I'd ever seen her try before.

"Your hair is different too!" I exclaimed. "You're all making me feel like I actually *have* been away for a month."

"Maybe we did it on purpose," Frida teased. "So you'll think twice about going away and leaving us again."

My stomach did a little drop as I thought about just that: leaving the Kicks for good and moving back to Connecticut. I knew for sure now that I didn't want to go. I wanted to stay in California with my friends. I thought back to my first few days at Kentville Middle School. If someone had told me I could move back home, I would've jumped at the chance. But so much had changed. This was my home now, and I loved all of my new friends.

"Anyway," Frida continued. "We want to hear all about your trip!"

"Definitely," I said. "But first—"

I took out the beaded bracelets I'd gotten for everybody.

"Supercute!" Zoe said, slipping hers on, and then the rest of us put ours on, because I'd gotten one for myself, too.

"We match! They're kind of like friendship bracelets," Emma remarked.

"I hadn't thought of that," I said. "But yeah, you're right."

Then we started to eat. Emma's bento box was filled with yummy Korean food her mom had made. Jessi had bought her lunch from the cafeteria; no wonder, with the new baby at home keeping everyone busy. Frida and Zoe had brown bagged it, and so had I. My mom had made me my favorite turkey wrap, with avocado and tomatoes.

"How was the trip?" Frida asked. "We need deets."

"It was, well . . ." I tried to find the right word. "Weird. It was weird between me and Kara." And then the entire story came spilling out. About Kara and the Ruesters. How Sienna had not been very nice to me. How the whole trip was not what I had been expecting.

"Who exactly is this Sienna?" Frida asked.

"I didn't know her. She came from a different elementary school," I explained. "She and Kara met in middle school. And now, from the sound of it, they're inseparable. Sleepover parties, working out together, going out with all my old friends from elementary school. I felt like an outsider."

"Hmmmmmm . . ." Frida frowned. "The bottom line is, you don't know much about her, right?"

"Yes, that's true," I admitted. "Except for the fact that for some reason she doesn't like me very much."

"Maybe she's jealous," Emma suggested. "Or feels threatened by you because you and Kara are such good friends."

I almost said, *What does she have to be jealous about? I live all the way across the country!* but then stopped myself. That might not be true for long. And I couldn't bring myself to tell my friends there was a possibility I might move. So I changed the subject.

"Where is the nugget photo spectacular I've been promised?" I asked, which prompted Jessi to grab her phone and start scrolling through what seemed like a million pics of her adorable baby brother.

"And there he is with the teddy bear I got him," she said, pointing at one photo of Oliver in the hospital bassinet, lying next to a soft and cuddly brown toy bear.

"That bear is bigger than he is!" Zoe said.

Jessi laughed. "He'll grow into it. At least that's what my mom said."

As we chatted and looked at pics of Oliver, I couldn't help but wonder if I'd be around to see him get bigger and grow up. I silently sighed to myself. This was torture!

• • •

On the soccer field at practice that afternoon, I was ready to relieve some stress and get ready for our first playoff game.

"Welcome back, Devin!" Coach Flores called out to me as the team was doing warm-up laps around the field. "I see you brought some speed back with you!"

With that, I turned and noticed that I was half a lap ahead of the rest of the team.

"Devin, wait up!" Jessi called.

"Where's the fire?" Grace asked me.

I jogged in place, waiting for Jessi to catch up.

"Maybe you should try out for the track team," Jessi suggested when she caught up to me, panting slightly. "You seem ready to do the forty-yard dash."

"It just feels good to run," I told her. "Especially after being stuck on an airplane for hours."

Jessi nodded. "I know what you mean. Nobody tells you that waiting for someone to have a baby is really boring. You just sit around a dumb hospital waiting room, and wait, wait, and oh yeah, then you get to wait some more. And after the baby is born, more waiting. Mostly for him to wake up and do something interesting."

"We'll just have to bring all that excess energy we have stored up onto the soccer field," I said, and we got our chance as we broke into two teams for a scrimmage.

It was clear that both Jessi and I were high energy, but also clear that neither of us was very focused.

Grace sent a pass to me on my left, and I went right. I went offsides twice in the scrimmage.

Jessi intercepted a pass from one of her own team members and fumbled another pass.

"Jessi! Devin!" Grace yelled. "Where are your heads?"

Jessi shrugged sheepishly. "In baby mode. Sorry, Grace."

My mode was "worried about having to move back to Connecticut," but I couldn't say that.

"I'll get it together," I said instead.

"You'd better!" Grace said firmly. "Our first playoff game is Saturday, and we have never beaten the Eagles in the regular season. If you play like that, we won't stand a chance."

I gulped. Grace was right. Being the best at soccer meant everything to me. I couldn't let Sienna, or the thought of moving, put me off my game. I had to be ready to win this Saturday!

CHAPTER NINE

"Here he is, our Oliver." Mrs. Dukes beamed as she placed the baby into my arms. He had a slight covering of brown fuzz on top of his head, and he was sound asleep. His eyes were shut tight, and his tiny little upturned nose was a teeny bit wrinkled.

"He's adorable," I said admiringly as I sat on the couch in Jessi's living room, looking down at the baby. I'd had to wash my hands thoroughly and then put on some hand sanitizer before I could hold him.

"He's little and we don't want him catching a cold," Jessi had explained to me firmly. I had gone to her house after school on Tuesday, since we didn't have soccer practice. It was funny to see Jessi, usually the first to crack a joke, be so serious about her little brother.

As I held him, I noticed the writing on his little green onesie: DADDY AND MOMMY'S MIRACLE.

"His onesie is so sweet," I said to Mrs. Dukes.

She smiled. "It's true. After we had Jessi, I was told I wouldn't be able to have any more children. And then suddenly, out of the blue, came Oliver! He is a true miracle."

"You probably needed twelve years to rest after giving birth to me," Jessi told her mom. "After all, making this kind of perfection"—she gestured at herself—"can take a lot out of a person."

Mrs. Dukes and I laughed. Then Jessi's mom stopped suddenly.

"Oh dear," she said. "If Oliver is anything like Jessi, I'm in trouble. She was early to walk and talk."

"I'll have him speaking in no time." Jessi leaned over me and tickled Oliver's tummy with one finger. "His first word will be 'Jessi.' Just wait and see."

Oliver, reacting to Jessi's touch, moved his head from side to side in my arms. Then his tiny little rosebud lips opened and he gave a sweet baby sigh.

"Oh, that face!" I exclaimed. "I don't remember Maisie being this cute."

"Well, you were much younger when Maisie was born," Mrs. Dukes said.

"I guess," I said. "But I know that she cried all the time, and it totally annoyed me. Actually, not much has changed!"

"Oh, come on. Maisie isn't that bad," Jessi replied.

I gave her a look as I raised an eyebrow. "Would you trade Oliver for her?"

"No way!" Jessi exclaimed. "Okay, point taken."

We laughed, but then I remembered Maisie's reaction to the stuffed *T. rex*. And reading to her at bedtime when she was little. And doing soccer drills in the backyard together.

"Actually, I wouldn't trade Maisie for Oliver," I said. "No offense. I mean, he's adorable. But you're right . . . she's not that bad."

Oliver began to stir again, this time opening his mouth and giving a slight, mewling cry, kind of like a cat.

"I'll take him," Mrs. Dukes said as she scooped him up out of my arms. "It's time for him to eat. You girls go ahead and help yourselves to a snack in the kitchen."

Jessi pulled out some cheese, wheat crackers, and grapes, and we munched on them together.

"Ugh. We really blew it at soccer practice yesterday, didn't we?" Jessi said.

I sighed. "Yep. My head was off in the clouds."

"I know. Mine was too," Jessi said. "All I could think about was Oliver. What he was doing, if he was sleeping. Remember how freaked out I was at first when I found out my mom was having a baby? I was miserable!"

I nodded. "Yep, and when you had to give up your room."

Jessi had had to move from her room on the second floor with her parents to a smaller room on the first floor. She had not been happy about it.

"I wasn't excited to be a big sister at all. But seeing him, and holding him, I can't believe how much I love him. It kicked in right away. I never thought of myself as a baby person before," she said.

"And you are now?" I asked.

"I am a one-baby person," she replied. "Oliver. He's special. And I'm going to look out for him."

I smiled. "He is so lucky to have you as a big sister."

"True," Jessi said with a grin. "But anyway, Oliver is why I couldn't concentrate at practice. It doesn't explain why Devin, who has a soccer ball for a brain, couldn't concentrate."

"Maybe I was still jet-lagged," I said. "And I don't like it that things are weird between me and Kara. Plus, I have something else on my mind . . ." I trailed off.

"What is it? Come on, Devin. You can tell me." Jessi had her hands on her hips, and I knew I wouldn't get out of there without spilling it.

So I told her about overhearing my dad on the phone at the hotel, and how I thought we might have to move back to Connecticut.

Jessi's eyes grew wide. "No way! That would stink so bad. I can't even!"

"I know. Me too. I love you guys and I don't want to leave," I told Jessi.

"You can stay here with us. I know my bedroom is really small, but we can make it work," Jessi said.

"I don't think my parents would want that," I said. "But thanks. I appreciate it."

Jessi looked sad. "I need you! I don't want you to go."

"I don't want to go either," I said.

Jessi bit her lip, thinking. "Maybe it won't happen. Or maybe you heard wrong."

I had thought that was possible too. "You could be right," I said, just as my phone beeped that I had a text. It was my dad, who was waiting for me outside.

"I gotta go," I told Jessi. "I'll see you tomorrow. And you're right, Oliver is a very special baby. He is a whole new level of cuteness."

"He gets it from his big sister." Jessi laughed.

When I got home, I raced upstairs to my bedroom. Kara and I had a weekly video chat every Tuesday at this time, and I didn't want to be late.

I logged in to the video chat software. It rang and rang, but Kara never picked up the call.

That's weird, I thought. *If she ever has to miss a call, she lets me know.* My next thought made my whole stomach sink. *What if she saw it was me calling and didn't pick up because she didn't want to talk to me?*

Troubled, I went downstairs to set the table for dinner, one of my daily chores. Dad usually did the cooking, but tonight Mom was in the kitchen, whirring something in the food processor.

"Hey, Devin," she said as she added some artichokes to the mixture. "How's little Oliver doing?"

I shrugged, unable to say anything. I felt like I might

burst into tears. I was confused and upset about everything.

"Aw, sweetie." My mom shut off the food processor and wrapped her arms around me. "What's the matter?"

I took a deep breath, trying to calm myself.

"I think Kara hates me!" I blurted out.

"Come, sit down." Mom guided me to the kitchen table, and I took a seat. She sat next to me and held my hand. "Tell me about it."

"Kara was just really different when I saw her. She kept getting mad at me. And she has this new friend who doesn't like me. It was all very strange, and I felt like I didn't belong there anymore. And how can I move back to Connecticut if Kara won't be my friend? All my other friends have changed. It's not the same."

My mom looked at me, surprise registering on her face.

"What makes you think we're moving to Connecticut?" she asked.

"I heard Dad talking on the phone at the hotel," I admitted. "I wasn't eavesdropping. I just couldn't help hearing what he was saying."

Mom patted my shoulder. "Don't worry. I know you wouldn't eavesdrop, Devin. But overhearing parts of other people's conversations can cause problems and confusion. You should have said something to me or your dad."

"I was too afraid. When we first got here, part of me kind of wanted to move back home. But now, after all these months, and as things got worse and worse with

Kara, I got scared that we *would* move. And that maybe it would be terrible."

"Oh, you poor thing," Mom said. "Carrying all that around inside you. Well, let me tell you, we are *not* moving back to Connecticut. Your dad was offered an opportunity to transfer. We discussed it and decided that we were happy here and things were working out well for us and you girls. And we've both fallen in love with Southern California, so we are staying put."

I felt my shoulders relax as a wave of relief passed through my body. I didn't realize until then how tense and tight every muscle had been.

"I love it here too," I said. "I'm glad we're staying. But I still want to patch things up between me and Kara. How can I do that if I don't even know what went wrong in the first place?"

"You have to talk to her and be honest about what you're feeling," Mom said. "I know it's scary to do that, but you'll feel so much better when you get everything out in the open."

I nodded. My mom was right. But how could I fix things with Kara if she wouldn't even talk to me?

CHAPTER TEN

The next morning I was still feeling down about Kara. It wasn't like her to ignore me when I tried to contact her, even when we were mad at each other. We'd fought a bunch of times before, but we'd always talked it out.

Kara's behavior was a real mystery, but what I didn't know was that detective Frida was on the case. At lunch time I learned all about it.

Frida plopped her tray down next to me at our cafeteria table and took a seat.

"Devin, we need to talk," she said. "I have some very important information for you."

"Um, okay," I said, a little bit nervously. Frida sounded super serious!

"That friend of Kara's has been spreading misinformation about you on social media, and I have the proof!" she said.

"Wait, what?" I asked. "You mean Sienna?"

Frida nodded. "Yes, Sienna. And I can promise you, this is going to be shocking."

"Oooooh!" Emma squealed. "This sounds juicy."

"Definitely!" Zoe agreed, leaning across the table.

"Excuse me," I said, "but we're talking about my life here. This is not some reality show."

"Sorry," Emma said. "It's just, Frida makes everything sound so exciting."

Jessi nodded. "She does. Frida would be great on a reality show."

Frida sniffed. "Reality shows are an insult to the craft of acting. There's no way I would do a reality show."

"What about competition shows?" Zoe said. "Those are fun, and they show off people's skills. I'd love to do a fashion design show, maybe, if I get better at sewing."

I thought my head was going to explode. "Can we please get back to Frida's news?" I asked. "I'm dying of curiosity."

"Okay, okay," Frida said. "Let me start at the beginning. Do you remember Diana Diego?"

I frowned. "Diana Diego? I don't think so."

Frida held up her phone and showed me a picture of a girl with brown hair in two braids and black-framed eyeglasses. It came back to me.

"That's the disguise you used when we were trying to prove that the Rams had sabotaged us!" I cried.

Emma scooted around the table to look. "Let me see!"

"I remember that," Jessi chimed in. "Frida pretended to be a new student who wanted to join the Rams, and she got one of the players to admit to the sabotage."

That was all true. In the fall season the Rams had done stuff like poking holes in our soccer balls and defacing our team banner. Their team captain had been under a lot of pressure to win, and she had orchestrated it all. Frida's disguise had uncovered their final plan: to make it look like we had spray painted "Kicks Rule" on our own field, which would have made us forfeit the game. Thanks to Frida, we were able to stop the Rams, and we went on to win the game.

"What does Diana Diego have to do with Sienna?" I asked.

"When I became Diana Diego, I created a Snapface account," Frida explained. "I requested Sienna as a friend on Snapface, and she accepted right away. I started scrolling through her posts, and I found this one from three days ago."

Frida handed me her phone, and I looked at a post from Sienna that she'd made on the day I flew back to California. It was one of those posts that was cryptic unless you knew who the person was talking about.

Sad when your friend's friend talks behind her back and you can't do anything about it.

There were a few replies from girls with question marks, or basic statements of agreement. Then I saw a reply from Kara.

Wait, which friend?

You, Sienna replied.

The back-and-forth went like this:

Kara: You mean Devin?

Sienna: Yes.

Kara: What do you mean? What did she say?

Sienna: I don't want to hurt ur feelings.

Kara: Tell me!

Sienna: At the practice. She told me she liked her friends back home more than u.

Kara: She didn't!

Sienna: I was shocked.

Kara: ☹

"I never said that!" I cried.

"I'm sure you didn't," Frida said.

"I barely even talked to her at the practice," I said. "I mean, we talked for a little bit, but I never said that I liked you guys better than I like Kara. You know that I love you all equally."

"Well, you like me a little better than everyone else, but that's understandable," Jessi joked, and I nudged her.

"No wonder Kara doesn't want to talk to me," I said. "If Sienna made up this lie on Snapface, who knows what else she's been telling Kara?"

"Exactly!" Frida said, and then pounded her fist on the table for emphasis.

"Can you screen shot that for me?" I asked.

"Already done," Frida said. "I'm sending it to you now."

"Thanks," I said.

"That's weird, that Sienna would try to sabotage your friendship with Kara like that," Zoe remarked.

"She must be really insecure about her relationship with Kara," Emma guessed.

"Maybe," I said thoughtfully. Sienna's lie explained a lot. But something was bugging me. Why was Kara so ready to believe her?

"Well, anyway. Thanks, Detective Frida!" I said.

"No problem," she replied.

"I'm glad Frida figured this out, because we need your head in the game on Saturday," Jessi said. "Our first play-off game!"

"I still have to talk to Kara," I said. "But don't worry. I'm psyched for the playoffs."

Jessi grinned. "Let's kill it at practice today, okay?"

"Definitely," I said. "No more excuses!"

And when it came time for practice that afternoon, I kept my promise. I pushed the Kara problem out of my mind and gave my all to every drill. During the scrimmage I managed to steal the ball twice, and I scored three goals. I was on fire!

"Looking good out there today, Dev," said Grace as we all walked off the field after practice. "If you play like that on Saturday, the Eagles won't know what hit them."

"Can you pass some of that energy on to the rest of us?" teased Megan.

I grinned. "You don't need mine. We're all going to bring it on Saturday."

"We're going to need to," Grace said. "We haven't beaten the Eagles yet."

Jessi chimed in. "Yeah, you keep saying that. You're going to jinx us!"

I was kind of glad Jessi mentioned it. Grace usually wasn't a negative person. I got the feeling that she wanted to win the playoffs badly, and the Eagles thing was psyching her out.

"I'm just stating a fact, Jessi," Grace said.

"We'll be on our home field this time, so that should help," Megan pointed out.

"Yeah, but I hear their defense has gotten even better," Grace countered.

"Maybe, but we came out of the season with a better record than them," Megan argued. "We've got this."

"Let's hope so," Grace said, and she sounded a little unsure.

By now every other member of the team had quieted down and was listening to Grace and Megan. Grace noticed.

"But, hey, there's nothing to worry about!" she said. "We're going to beat the Eagles this time. We're going to move forward in the playoffs."

"YEAH!" Jessi called out loudly, leading us all to burst out in a spontaneous cheer.

"Goooooooo, Kicks!"

But everyone walked off the field more slowly than usual, and I could tell that Grace's fears had gotten everyone a little rattled.

On the way home from practice, I texted Kara.

Home in 20 minutes. Can we video chat? Please? It's really important!

I waited a good ten minutes for Kara to reply, and all I got was: K.

That was enough! When I got home, I bolted up the stairs and turned on my laptop. I listened to the beeps as I waited for Kara to pick up. Would she do it, or would she ignore me again?

To my relief, the screen opened up and I saw her face.

"Kara, Sienna lied to you!" I blurted out.

Kara frowned. "If you're just going to bash Sienna—"

"No. I said this was important." I held up my phone with the screen shot and showed her. "I never, ever said that I liked my California friends better than you. I would *never* say that! You know how it is. I love you all in different ways."

"What, you're snooping on Sienna's profile now?" Kara asked.

"Not me. Frida," I said.

"That's right. Your *new* friend Frida," Kara said, pouting.

I sighed. "Come on, Kara. You've got to believe me. I would never say anything like that about you. You know that."

Kara hesitated. "I guess."

"You and I have been best friends *forever*," I went on. "Since pre-K, when we painted each other's faces and Miss Horner freaked out. Since that Halloween when we both dressed up as Belle and told everybody we were twins. Since that day I got stung by a bee at your house and you held my hand until it felt better. That's all real, Kara, and nobody can take that away from us."

Kara's face softened. She smiled. "Miss Horner was *so* mad. I just wanted to give you a cat face like I'd gotten at the carnival."

"See?" I said. "We've got history, Kara. And that will never change. No matter where I live, or how many other friends I make. You will always be my Kara."

"And you'll always be my Devin," she said.

We were both quiet for a minute, and then Kara spoke up.

"But you need to stop trash-talking Sienna," she said. "She's my friend now."

I nodded. "I get it," I said. Then I held up the phone again. "I'm just saying, this is shady. But I understand. I think maybe Sienna is jealous of our friendship, which is ridiculous. I mean, I live all the way across the country! And she gets to see you every day. If anything, *I* should be jealous of her."

Kara smiled. "You mean that?"

"Of course!" I said. "In a perfect world, you would live here with me in California, and I'd have all of my friends in one place. But I don't. And I miss you a lot."

"I miss you too," Kara admitted. "And I talk about you all the time. I mean, *all* the time, to everyone."

"That's probably why Sienna is jealous, then," I guessed.

Kara nodded. "That makes sense."

"So you believe me?" I asked.

"Yes," Kara replied. "I believe you. And I'm sorry I believed Sienna so easily."

"That's okay," I said, but inside I was still a little worried. How strong was our friendship, really, if Kara had given up on me that quickly?

Or maybe this was just a regular thing that happened when your friends were far away. Sometimes you got lost; sometimes you got knocked off the friendship seesaw, but you could always climb back on again if you had help.

We talked some more, about regular things this time, and then Mom called me down to dinner.

"Good luck on Saturday," Kara said.

"Thanks!" I said. "Good luck with your game this weekend too."

"Gooooo, Kicks!" Kara cheered as we were both hanging up, and it made me feel good. I was glad that Kara was still in my life. And I was happy that I had friends like Jessi, Frida, Emma, and Zoe, too!

CHAPTER ELEVEN

"I know some of you are worried that we haven't beaten the Victorton Eagles yet," Coach Flores began her pep talk before Saturday's game. "And I'm here to tell you why that doesn't matter."

Every member of the Kicks stared at Coach Flores hopefully. At Friday's practice all anybody had talked about was "the unstoppable Eagles." I'm not sure who had dubbed them that, although I suspected it was Frida being dramatic, as usual. We had all left practice convinced that the Eagles couldn't be beat, just like at the practice on Wednesday.

"It doesn't matter because every game is a fresh start," Coach said. "It wouldn't matter if the Eagles had beaten us twenty times! The only thing that matters is how we play today. And today we're going to win!"

Emma raised her hand. "Do you really think they could beat us twenty times?" she asked.

"No, that's not—" Coach sighed. "Listen, girls, I'm getting the idea that you're psyching yourselves out for this game, and you need to shake it off. You've worked hard for this, and you're playing better than I've ever seen you. We've got a full team and we're ready to roll. Nobody's suspended. Nobody's injured. Nobody's . . ."

Frida ran away from the circle and rapped her knuckles against the nearest tree.

"Frida, what are you doing?" Coach asked.

"Knocking on wood," she said. "We don't want to tempt fate. All it takes is for somebody to trip over a shoelace, or for a rabid groundhog to storm the field—"

"Okay, none of those things are going to happen," Coach said. "Please come back here."

Frida dutifully jogged back, and I heard Jessi whisper, "A rabid groundhog?" Then she burst into giggles.

"You never know," Frida whispered back.

"That's who you should be on the field," I joined in. "A rabid groundhog."

Frida's eyes lit up. "Yes!"

"All right. We've got ten minutes till game time," Coach said. "Do your sock swap, and then let's get on some dribbling drills."

"Yes, Coach!" we all called out.

We immediately formed a circle on the grass and sat down. Each person took off their right sock and passed it to the person on the right. Jessi was on my left, and she handed me a sock with little trucks on it.

"I bought a toy dump truck for Oliver," she told me. "But

I have to wait until he's three months old to give it to him."

"You are such a good big sister!" I said. "I didn't get Maisie a present when she was born."

"It's not too late," Jessi teased.

I glanced up into the stands. There was Mom and Dad with Maisie, who was holding a GO, DEVIN! sign she had made herself with markers and glitter. I felt a surge of warmth for all three of them. I had the best family. They were always there to cheer me on!

"Welcome to the first game in the girls' middle school soccer championships!"

I jumped a little at the sound of the announcer. Because this was a playoff game, Kentville Middle School had gone all out to let us play on the school's main field (otherwise known as the boys' field). They'd asked Mr. Ahmadi, the football announcer, to call the game.

"All rise for the National Anthem!"

We quickly laced up and ran to the sidelines, where we stood in a line while our middle school band played the anthem. Then Mr. Ahmadi announced the starting lineup for the Eagles, and the girls ran out onto the field one at a time.

I sized them up as they ran out, and I knew my teammates were doing it too. The Eagles looked like average soccer players in their red-and-yellow uniforms, not the scary super athletes we had imagined we were facing. I started to feel confident, like maybe we could finally beat them.

"And now for the starting lineup of the Kentville

Kangaroos!" Mr. Ahmadi announced, totally ignoring that everyone knew us as the Kicks. "Co-captain Grace Kirkland . . . co-captain Devin Burke . . ."

I ran out onto the field to join Grace, to the sounds of the crowd cheering in the stands.

I could get used to being announced at the start of every game, I thought.

I looked down at the Kicks starters, and everyone was smiling. Me, Grace, and Megan were forwards. Jessi, Zoe, Taylor, and Maya were in the midfield. Frida, Jade, and Giselle were defending, and Emma was on goal. I was psyched to see all of my besties starting with me.

"And finally, the coach for the Kangaroos, Coach Flores!" Mr. Ahmadi announced.

We all clapped for our coach, the ref tossed a coin, and Grace called heads.

The coin landed on tails, and the Eagles chose to attack.

That's okay, I thought. *We're ready for them!*

The Eagles' forward pivoted and passed the ball to a midfielder. She dribbled it and passed it back to the forward. The forward kicked a long pass, but Jessi intercepted it! I ran ahead of her as she dribbled down the field, speeding into Eagles territory. Were we heading toward our first score?

But in her speed, Jessi kicked the ball out of bounds. One of the Eagles tossed it in, and another Eagle stopped it with her feet. She kicked a short pass, and I intercepted it. I saw Zoe open down the field, so I kicked it high and hard to her.

Wham! Zoe headed the ball, and it flew to Maya, who

took off like a rocket. But just like Jessi, she veered too close to the sideline, and the ball went out of bounds.

An Eagles player threw the ball in to another Eagle, who dribbled it right into our goal zone. Frida ran up to her.

"I'm wild and I'm dangerous! I'm a rabid groundhog!" she cried, trying to get the ball from the offense. The Eagles player, number five, wasn't fazed at all. She turned her back to Frida and skillfully dribbled the ball away from her and passed it to another player.

Then the Eagles sent the ball zigzagging around the field like a pinball, making quick, short passes from one player to another. Finally one of the Eagles broke away and sped toward our goal.

Jade charged her and kicked the ball away, sending it over our own goal line—the end of the field to the right of the goal net. The Eagles player took the ball to the corner for a corner kick, and I was starting to feel anxious. There was too much activity near our goal. We needed to keep the ball on the Eagles' side!

The Eagles kicked the ball back onto the field, and all our defenders scrambled, trying to get control of it. Giselle kicked it out of the way of one of the Eagles and sent it over our goal line again. The Eagles made another corner kick and once again both teams scrambled for control. Frida got the ball and kicked it to Zoe, who was open, but one of the Eagles swooped in and got to it before Zoe could. The Eagles player zoomed right up to the goal and kicked it in before Emma knew what was happening.

The Eagles fans erupted into cheers, and I could feel my

stomach sink. The Eagles had scored first. That wasn't a good sign.

It doesn't mean anything, I told myself. *We can come back from this!*

The ball returned to the center of the field, and Grace kicked it to Megan—but number five came from out of nowhere and intercepted it. She dribbled it fast—too fast—and the ball bounced away from her, out of bounds.

Zoe threw it in to Jessi, who bounced the ball off her chest and down to her feet. She tried to pass it to me, but an Eagles player ran in front of me and kicked the ball out of bounds.

I threw the ball in to Megan, and when she tried to pass it to Grace, the Eagles intercepted it. They passed it from one player to another and got past our defenders and shot it into the goal. I saw the look of anguish on Emma's face as the ball soared past her, and I felt for her.

I had remembered that the Eagles had great defense, but they must have been working on their offensive game too. We couldn't keep up with their passing, and by the end of the first half, the score was Kicks 0, Eagles 5.

Coach Flores called us into a huddle at the sideline. Everyone was quiet and looked miserable. We were all thinking the same thing: We were never going to make it past the first game.

"I know what you're thinking," Coach said. "There's no way to come back from this. But there is."

"But they're five points ahead of us!" Anjali pointed out.

"And we can't score," Taylor added.

"We *can* score," Coach said. "You guys have scored dozens of times this season. You know how to score."

She turned to Grace. "What do you think was happening during the first half?"

"Well, they intercepted us a lot," Grace said.

Coach nodded. "Right. What else?"

Jessi raised her hand. "We lost control of the ball more than usual."

"That's true," Coach said. "So I want to see more control out there. Make sure your teammate is clear before you pass the ball. Forwards, when you get the ball, do what you do best. Get it past their defense. You can do it. I *know* you can do it. I believe in you. Now come on, let's hear it!"

"Let's get fired up!" Grace chanted. Then she clapped four times.

We repeated her.

"Let's get fired up!" C*lap, clap, clap, clap.*

"Let's get fired up!" she cheered again. C*lap, clap, clap, clap.*

"Let's get fired up!" C*lap, clap, clap, clap.*

"LET'S GET FIRED UP!" C*lap, clap, clap, clap.*

"LET'S GET FIRED UP!" C*lap, clap, clap, clap.*

We finished with a loud whoop!

Coach benched me for the start of the second half—no matter what the score was, she liked to give everyone a chance to play. I sat next to Emma and Jessi and bounced my leg up and down, watching the action on the field.

Maybe we weren't going to win, but right from the start of this half, it was clear that we weren't going to give up, either. We had control of the ball, and Grace passed it to Brianna, who passed it to Olivia, who passed it back to Grace. Then Grace charged the goal like a bull and blew the ball right past the goalie. The Kicks had scored their first point!

I leaped to my feet. The Kicks stands erupted in cheers. This wasn't over yet!

A wave of energy swept across the Kicks players on the field. We got control of the ball again after the Eagles sent it out of bounds, and this time Zoe scored after a pass from Grace. We were catching up!

Minutes later the Eagles broke through our defense again, but Zarine, our other goalkeeper, jumped and caught the ball. She tossed it in to Jade, who kicked it to Olivia, who took it as far as she could and passed it to Grace. Then Grace made another goal, bringing the score to Kicks 3, Eagles 5.

"I told you that you knew how to score!" Coach Flores called out, with a big grin on her face. As the ball changed teams, she put me, Emma, and Jessi back in. I practically bounced onto the field. I was so eager to get in there and prove that I could score too!

I got my first chance when one of the Eagles passed the ball and it skidded right past me. I got my foot on it and then dribbled down the field. I couldn't see anybody open, so I just kept going.

With the goal in sight, I kicked it hard and high. It sailed over the goalie's right shoulder . . .

Whomp! It sank into the net! Jessi high-fived me. Panting, I raced back to the midfield.

"That was Devin Burke, scoring for the Kangaroos," Mr. Ahmadi announced over the speakers. "Now Kentville is one point shy of tying up this game."

A new energy seemed to infect the Eagles, too, and the next few minutes on the field were tense. They intercepted us. We intercepted them. We traded the ball back and forth in the midfield, and nobody managed to break away into the other team's goal zone.

Then the Eagles *did* break away—player number 5 was at it again, using fancy footwork to outstep our defenders. She did get a shot at the goal, but the ball went out of bounds. Jade tossed it to Jessi, who took it toward the midfield. I got open so she could pass it to me, and then I passed it to Grace. One of the Eagles defenders ran in front of Grace and kicked the ball out of the way, over the Eagles goal line and at the end of the field, a few feet from the edge of the net. Now it was our turn to take a corner kick!

Grace took the ball into the corner and passed it to me. Two defenders charged me, but I ran between them and kicked the ball into the goal.

Whomp! Right through the goalie's legs.

I jumped up and down.

"And the score is tied," Mr. Ahmadi said. "With four minutes left in the game, either one of these teams could be moving on in the playoffs."

"And it's going to be us," said Grace as she jogged past me. There was a determination on her face that I'd never seen before, and I loved it.

The Eagles had the ball again, and number five kicked it sideways to another one of her team's forwards. That player dribbled it down the field, taking long steps, and Zoe zipped in and took the ball as it skidded down the grass in front of the Eagles forward. The Eagles player tried to get it back, but Zoe had better footwork than even number five did, and she broke away. She kicked the ball high to Megan, who headed it to Jessi, who passed it to Grace.

As soon as Grace got into scoring range, the Eagles defenders charged her. Thinking quickly, she kicked the ball high over their heads. I held my breath as the ball soared over the grass . . . Had she aimed too high?

Whomp! She hadn't! Grace had scored! We were up by one point!

"And that was Grace Kirkland, scoring for the Kangaroos," Mr. Ahmadi said. "Excuse me. I've been told that the team is known as the Kicks. So the score is Kicks 6, Eagles 5. The Eagles need to score in these last few minutes to tie up the game."

The Kentville stands had erupted into a chant.

Stomp-stomp-clap! "Kicks will win!" *Stomp-stomp-clap!* "Kicks will win!"

My heart was pounding as I took my place in the midfield. I noticed that number five was still in as a forward, and she was starting to slow down a little bit. But she had the same look of determination on her face that I had seen on Grace's, and I knew we had to watch out for her.

I was right. Number five was determined to score. She passed the ball to one of her teammates and then raced toward the Kicks goal. Emma stood, ready, gloved hands on her knees, as the Eagles passed the ball closer and closer.

One of the Eagles stormed the goal, and it looked like she was going to try to score. Frida and Jade descended on her. But she surprised everyone by passing the ball backward to number five, who had a clear shot. Number five kicked it hard and fast to the extreme left side of the net. Emma had been on the right side, expecting the shot from the other player.

We're going to tie, I thought. *This isn't over yet.*

But then Emma did one of the sideways jumps she'd been practicing. Because she was so tall, her arms were very long, and when she jumped, she extended them as far as they could go. Her fingers gripped the ball, and she hugged it to her chest as her body fell to the ground.

The stands erupted again.

"That was a very nice save by Emma Kim of the Kicks," Mr. Ahmadi said.

I quickly ran to Emma to high-five her. She was grinning like a six-year-old at a birthday party.

"That was pretty good, right?" she asked.

"It was awesome!" I said, and then I jogged back up to the midfield.

The Kicks had control of the ball, but we didn't get far with it before the ref's whistle blew.

"And the game is over!" Mr. Ahmadi announced. "Kentville wins! The Kicks are advancing in the championship!"

We all quickly lined up to congratulate the Eagles on a good game.

And then we went wild, screaming and cheering. Emma hugged me. Jessi grabbed me by the arms, and we jumped up and down. I could see Kentville fans climbing down from the bleachers and running onto the field.

I heard Coach Flores over the cheering.

"Great job, girls! I knew you could do it!"

Jessi shook me. "Can you believe it? We're advancing!"

"I know!" I said. It was almost too hard to believe. We were two more games away from winning the championship. When my family had moved to California, I'd never dreamed that I'd get a chance to play on such a good team.

Emma, Frida, and Zoe joined me and Jessi in a group hug.

"We're going to take it all the way!" Emma cried.

"Do you think I should be a rabid groundhog again in the next game?" Frida asked. "It worked this time."

"Be whatever you want, Frida," Zoe told her. "Be Godzilla with a toothache or a zombie monkey or a fairy dragon princess. Just as long as you keep playing like you do."

I grinned. I'd also never dreamed that I would make such good friends, either!

I guess California was where I was meant to be.

TURN THE PAGE FOR A SNEAK PEEK AT
FANS IN THE STANDS

"Score! Rose Lavelle scores!" the announcer yelled. We were in Emma's movie room, and I jumped up from the couch, nearly knocking off Zoe, who was right next to me.

"Yes!" I pumped my fist into the air as the other players of the US Women's National Soccer team slapped Rose on the back in congratulations on Emma's practically-movie-screen-size television.

My best friend, Jessi, high-fived me. Some of the other Kicks were also there.

"We're winning!" Jessi crooned. Her hair, which she used to wear in long braids, was a mass of supercute black springy curls that shot out in all directions.

"Yes, but I'm gonna need to switch seats," Zoe chimed in. "Devin, you almost knocked over my drink!"

Zoe was the only one of us wearing a dress, but it was sporty—an off-the-shoulder black Adidas T-shirt dress, with cool white kicks. She was growing out her short hair, and it was starting to curl behind her ears. Zoe was always fashion forward.

"Oops, sorry!" I shrugged. "But you know how excited I get!"

Emma laughed. "I told my mom we should consider putting a tarp over the couches because of what happened last time."

I winced. During the World Cup the previous summer, in my excitement over the US women's team's win, I'd spilled red punch all over my seat. Mrs. Kim, Emma's mom, had been really nice about it, but I had been soooooo embarrassed.

"Don't remind me," I told Emma. She was the tallest of my friends and looked sporty too, with her long black hair pulled back into a ponytail, and a T-shirt with the emblem of the South Korean flag emblazoned in the middle of a soccer ball.

We were watching one of the games in the US Women's National Soccer team victory tour, after they'd won the World Cup. Today was a friendly match with Korea Republic, which was how FIFA, the International Federation of Association Football, referred to the South Korean women's team. Emma and her family were South Korean, and she debated over who to cheer for.

"Since it's a friendly game, I'm going to go ahead and root for Korea," she'd explained nervously when we'd first gotten to her house.

"Oh, don't worry, Devin," Emma said now as she threw an arm around my shoulder. "We'll just have to keep an eye on you. Maybe we should put you in the playroom for a little bit to calm down."

Emma's house was the perfect place to watch the game. It was more like a mansion than a house. The movie room was huge, with sliding glass doors leading out to the backyard, which had an in-ground pool. A large leather sectional surrounded the huge television screen, and there were comfy reclining chairs in place behind it. A long bar along the back wall had tall stools and every kind of soft drink we could imagine, including a new machine that poured out water or seltzer, and ten different fruit flavors we could add to it. Even though I could have had a soda, which I wasn't allowed to have at home, I loved trying all the different-flavored seltzers, so that was usually what I drank when I went to Emma's.

The playroom Emma was referring to was just down the hall from the movie room. It used to be for her and her brothers, but she had a large family with lots of little cousins, so they still used it all the time.

"When the nugget gets bigger, I'll have to bring him," Jessi said. The nugget was Jessi's newborn baby brother, Oliver, who was the cutest baby I'd ever seen. He was so happy and smiley, and almost never cried. Oliver was way different from my little sister, Maisie, who had screamed all the time when she was a baby. Now that she was eight, she could be okay sometimes, but I was glad earbuds had been invented, so I could tune her out when I needed to.

"There's a casting call for babies for a new line of organic baby food," Frida chimed in. "Your mom should take Oliver. He's a natural."

Frida was the only person I'd ever met in person who had been on TV. She was the same age as the rest of us, and played soccer too, but her true passion was acting. She'd been in a bunch of commercials. Her biggest role so far had been in *Mall Mania*, a TV movie that she'd costarred in with the singer Brady McCoy. She'd played his sister. Come to think of it, I guess Frida wasn't the only person I'd met who had been on TV, because she'd gotten Brady to show up for one of our soccer fundraisers, and we'd all gotten to meet him. He was really nice. Emma was a superfan, and I'd thought she was going to pass out, because she completely freaked out when she met him.

"I don't think my mom will go for that," Jessi said.

Frida shrugged. "Not everyone is called to be an actor," she said, a bit dramatically. Frida loved drama, and she loved to stand out, dressing in funky outfits and vintage clothing. Today she was toned down in yoga pants and a T-shirt, her long, reddish-brown hair falling in curls over her shoulders.

"That's true," Jessi said. "Who knows what Oliver will be like when he gets older? All he does now is sleep and eat. And speaking of eating—Emma, that soccer field snack stadium is amazing. And delicious!"

Emma beamed. "My mom and I worked on it all week," she said.

I joined Jessi as she went back to the table next to the bar where the food was set up. Emma and her mom had gone all out and re-created a soccer stadium, filling it with edible goodies.

The field was made out of guacamole, with soft white cheese piped onto it to make the boundary lines, and the goals made out of square pretzels. The back wall of the stadium had cute little American and South Korean flags with toothpick flagpoles.

Carrot sticks with olive heads looked like tiny soccer players on the field. Emma and her mom had cut up empty cereal boxes to make the stands and covered them with white paper and soccer ball stickers. The stands were filled with food: hot dogs, slider burgers, sushi, veggies, dip, potato chips, Cheez Doodles, cookies, candy, fruit, and popcorn. There were so many choices, I almost couldn't decide what to eat.

I filled a paper cup with M&M's and brought them back to the couch so I could snack on them while we watched the rest of the game. As I settled onto the sofa, Jessi sat next to me, with a plate piled high with sushi and potato chips.

"Mmm, sushi," Jessi said.

Zoe moved to the far end of the sectional away from me. "No offense, Devin, but this is a new dress, and I don't want to ruin it."

"It's only M&M's," I protested, holding my cup out and shaking it so she could see. With that, a cascade of the brightly colored candies came pouring out onto my lap.

Everyone started cracking up.

"See? I'm staying right here," Zoe said.

"Oh, Devin," Emma said as I scooped M&M's up from my lap and popped them into my mouth, "you might need to go into the playroom after all."

"I can't help it if you packed so many awesome things into the soccer snack stadium," I said.

"Maybe we can help you make another one, for when the Kicks win the championship," Jessi suggested.

"*If* we win the championship," I said.

"Yeah, don't jinx us, Jessi!" Frida cried.

My friends and I all played soccer for the Kentville Kangaroos, also known as the Kicks. We had made it to the playoffs for our spring season, and we'd won our first two playoff games. First we'd beaten the Victorton Eagles. And this morning we'd faced our longtime rivals, the Rams, on their turf, and had beaten them by just two points. We had only one more game before the final state championship match. It really felt like the win was in our grasp. Now, I wasn't as superstitious as Frida, but I definitely didn't want to spoil our chances either.

"Jessi's not jinxing us," Zoe countered. "We'll practice, we'll play, and we'll either win or lose."

"Thank you for sticking up for me, but don't even say the word *l-o-s-e*," Jessi said. "We're going to win!"

"Shhh," Emma said. "I think the game's coming back on."

But it wasn't the game—it was an ad for the US Men's National Soccer team game coming up next week. As we watched, Frida shook her head.

"It's *ridiculous* that the men get paid more than the women," she said. She'd taken lots of acting classes and knew how to put just the right oomph into anything she said.

I nodded my agreement. "The women's team has an amazing record in the World Cup—better than the men's team does."

"Yeah, they've won, like, four times," Jessi chimed in.

"But when France won the men's World Cup, they got something like thirty-eight million dollars," I said.

Frida tapped her phone screen and gasped. "When the US women's team came in first, they got only four million!"

"Wow, the men got, like—ten times more!" Jessi cried.

Frida fumed. "That's not all. Even in the regular season, the men make about three times as much as the women players. It's totally wrong."

"I heard there's a lawsuit so the players can get equal pay," Zoe commented.

"I hope the women win!" Jessi said. "Remember how the Kicks used to be treated compared to the boys' team? That was awful."

Emma's nodded in agreement. "We didn't even have a real soccer field, just dirt and weeds. We had trash cans as goalposts!"

"And while we were playing on that crummy field, the

boys had a real one to use," I said. "If Sally hadn't paid for ours to get renovated, we'd probably still be playing on dirt with garbage cans."

Sally Lane was the owner of a local sporting goods store. I hadn't thought about her for a while, but the Kicks really owed her a lot. Her confidence in the team had helped us gain more confidence in ourselves, and I definitely know that our playing improved when we weren't stepping into gopher holes. The new field was one of the things that had turned us from a last-place team into contenders for the championship!

"To Sally Lane!" Jessi said, holding a piece of sushi up in the air.

"To Sally Lane!" I said. I raised one of my M&M's to toast by touching it to Jessi's piece of sushi.

Everyone laughed as the game came back on the air. Both teams were good, but in the end, the US won.

"Oh, well." Emma pouted. "Maybe next time."

"Maybe the next World Cup will have South Korea and US in the final," I said, to cheer her up.

"That would be cool!" Emma said.

"And you can make your soccer snack stadium again for us," Jessi replied. "On second thought, I don't want to wait that long."

"It did take a lot of work," Emma said. "I think it will have to be for special occasions only."

I protested. "Hey, every time there's a soccer game is a special occasion."

Jessi laughed. "Soccer-ball-brain Devin."

As we waited for our parents to pick us up, Zoe pulled out her phone to show us her Instagram account.

"I started a new fashion account," she said, a little shyly.

We all oohed and aahed as we pulled out our phones to follow Zoe's new Insta. Her first post featured her oldest sister, Jayne, and was captioned "Working It." It featured Jayne in clothes for her new part-time job, as an office assistant in an accounting firm. She was hoping to be an accountant one day.

"I helped style Jayne for her new job," Zoe explained. "Then we took photos for fun, and Jayne had the idea for me to do a blog and link it to Instagram."

Jayne looked so grown-up and glamorous in the photos, I couldn't believe she was still a senior in high school.

"That's so awesome, Zoe!" I said, proud of my friend. When I had been in Connecticut for another friend's big sweet sixteen party, my luggage had gotten delayed by the airline, along with my party dress. Zoe had saved the day by sending the most beautiful gown at the last minute.

Zoe smiled. "Thanks. I'm really proud of it. I've asked Sabine to do a shoot for me, which would be cool because, besides the fact that she's gorgeous, we still haven't met in person yet. But her schedule's booked for a few weeks."

Sabine and I had met during my very brief modeling career. We'd stayed friends after I'd decided that modeling wasn't for me, and she and Zoe followed each other on social.

"Could you guys help me?" Zoe continued. "I'd interview you about your personal style and take some photos. It'll be really fun and easy, I promise."

Frida was in right away. "Of course!"

Jessi smiled and said, "Sure, why not? Although, I know I'm not as *gorgeous* as Sabine."

Zoe blushed. "You definitely are! But you know what I mean. Sabine is . . ."

"Stunning!" Frida finished for her. "But I'm not intimidated. I know how to make the camera fall in love with me."

"I'll do it," I said, but I was still thinking about Zoe's blush. Was she crushing on Sabine? If she was, that would make perfect sense. They had so much in common. I was about to ask her, when Emma spoke up.

"I wear jeans and T-shirts every day. It's like my uniform," she said. "I'm way too casual to be on a fashion blog."

Zoe shook her head. "You've got a great look, Emma, and I'll take care of helping you pick out what to wear. It'll be painless, I promise."

Easygoing Emma agreed. "Okay, you talked me into it!"

As our parents' cars started to arrive and we said goodbye, I reflected on how lucky I was to have such great friends. When I'd first come to California after moving from Connecticut, I had been really homesick. Then I'd met the Kicks, and everything had changed.

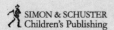

JOIN THIRD-GRADE SCIENTIST AND INVENTOR EXTRAORDINAIRE ADA LACE AS SHE SOLVES MYSTERIES USING SCIENCE AND TECHNOLOGY!